PRAISE FOR RODEO MAN

"If words were ragin' bulls, then Thadd Turner beat the eight second buzzer in bringing the reader the very essence of two-thousand-pound bulls with the hookin' horns and flyin' dirt that is bullfighting."

— MARK GREATHOUSE, MULTIPLE-AWARD-
WINNING WESTERN AUTHOR

"Rodeo Man is a fast-paced, action-packed story anyone in or out of the world of rodeo will enjoy. Filled with well-developed characters, Thadd Turner's "Rodeo Man" brings the reader face to face with the excitement and danger within the rodeo arena. I highly recommend this book, you won't want to put it down until the end."

— BILL MARKLEY, AUTHOR OF *THE LIFE AND
TIMES OF JIM BRIDGER*

RODEO MAN

RODEO MAN

THADD TURNER

WOLFPACK
PUBLISHING
— EST 2013 —

Rodeo Man
Paperback Edition
Copyright © 2025 by Thadd Turner

Wolfpack Publishing
1707 E. Diana Street
Tampa, FL 33610

www.wolfpackpublishing.com

Paperback ISBN 979-8-89567-794-0
Ebook ISBN 979-8-89567-805-3
LCCN 2025948044

This book is dedicated to the men and women who live the life of the rodeo professional and those aspiring to be champions. The story is inspired by the real guts and grit of the rodeo world. Special thanks to my family, wife Cindy, daughter Tanya, and son, Wyatt for your help and consideration in making this literary work the best it could be. Also, with gratitude to those who helped me write my first Western novel, The Hard Ride, a hard-driven action Western about legendary frontier scout and lawman Wild Bill Hickok.

And my sincere thanks to Wolfpack Publishing for their help and trust in me to deliver another great piece of entertaining material. With strong appreciation and support.

Thank you!
Thadd Turner
August 2025
Pass Christian, Mississippi

AUTHOR'S NOTE

This book is a work of fiction and fact pieced together to create an exciting story of genuine action and drama. Inspired by the modern-day rodeo cowboys and cowgirls of the Professional Cowboys Rodeo Association (PCRA) and the Professional Bull Riders, Inc. (PBR) and the many other regional rodeo events and organizations. The story takes us along for the last part of a bull rider's professional career, Daryl Weathers, who had a chance to be a champion bull rider like his father, but ignores the opportunity, not taking the sport seriously enough. He has a nemesis, Rex Winslow, whom he competes against, they dislike each other. Daryl has an opportunity to beat Rex at the Texas Regional Finals, the last competition before the World Championships, but is critically injured by a violent bull. Depressed and working back at his father's ranch in Texas, he drops to a new low, almost giving up on life, before discovering a new sport that is a natural fit for him, and he really likes—bullfighting.

He meets the love of his life, Christy, a pretty, blond cowgirl, who ironically is Rex's sister. Rex is furious and mad; he doesn't want his sister dating Daryl. Christy has an eight-year-old son, Cody, they both hit it off immediately together with Daryl. He begins his new journey into bullfighting at the local rodeo levels and then starts fighting like a professional cowboy at the larger events where he develops his new trademark "Slap Them Bulls!" Daryl slaps the rodeo bulls on the back side of their wide rumps with a white talcum powder handprint! Soon Daryl is offered the chance to fight the meanest bulls in the country at the World Championship Rodeo competition.

Daryl is amazing and is leading the points board in bullfighting through the final night of competition when he faces the meanest bull in the professional sport of rodeo—"Final Justice Rex," his former nemesis—the deadly two-thousand-pound beast of fury for his last ride. He sticks on the crazy bull for about seven seconds, then is violently thrown off and his hand stuck in the bull rope. The bull injures the two other bullfighters. Daryl is the last hope for Rex to survive the violent bull wreck and suddenly realizes that he must either decide to save himself and get out of the arena—or save the brother of the woman that he loves. The conflict now becomes the deadliest bullfight ever seen on dirt between man and beast!

RODEO MAN

1

BLOOD AND GUTS

OKLAHOMA CITY, 1996

THE AFTERNOON SUN BEATS DOWN HEAVILY ON AN OPEN
rodeo arena like warm punishment. The ninety-degree
heat ripples off the metal bleachers packed with eager
rodeo fans, all running high on cold beer and water,
heavy sweat, and jacked-up adrenaline. The crowd wears
a variety of cowboy hats, boots, tight jeans, short dresses,
and buttoned-up shirts with thin collars. A light breeze
blows the rodeo banners that flap indiscriminately from
every fence post around the rodeo arena. Outside the
arena and bleachers, the dirt parking lot is filled with
trucks and horse trailers, food and beer vendors, real
cowboys and cowgirls, and lots of smiling children. This
isn't just another rodeo stop, it's the last contest before
the National Finals World Championships, and everyone
feels the real pressure of success or failure.

A crackled voice blasts from the loudspeaker
attached above the bucking chutes. The rodeo

announcer, a man in his early forties, lean and gaunt, with short brown hair and a clean face, holds a well-worn microphone to his weathered lips: "Well, folks, it doesn't get any tougher for these bull riders than Oklahoma City! The last stop on the grueling road to the National Finals in Las Vegas!"

Down below in the bucking chutes, a young bull rider, early twenties, wide-brimmed hat tugged down low, sits strapped onto the back of a big brown Brahman bull. The rider adjusts his tight grip on the bull rope cinched in front of his lap. The chute boss, thirties, muscled with a potbelly, tightens the flank cinch strap under the big bull. The leather creaks and groans louder, rubbing against the bull's rough belly, the Brahma bull looks uncomfortable, he snorts louder and paws angrily at the ground, digging deeper—the young bull rider stares at the big bull then nods at the gate man.

"Let's go!"

The gate swings open. The chute explodes with heavy leather, angry fury, and wide horns. Two thousand pounds of flesh and bones launching skyward, jumping, twisting, kicking, snapping its head side to side like it's trying to tear apart the thick warm air itself, as it tries to unseat the young bull rider off its back. Chunks of arena dirt fly everywhere, and thick powdered dust fills the arena around the bull and rider, the crowd is roaring their approval loudly…

Standing and watching outside the arena fence, eight-year-old Daryl Weathers, thin, light-brown hair, regular height with a dark-gray cowboy hat over his head, leans against the safety of the railing. His eyes are wide with excitement, his hands tightly gripping the top rail above his head. The experienced cowboy beside him, his father,

Cal Weathers, mid-thirties, a rugged bull riding veteran of the arena with a tanned hardened face underneath a well-worn cowboy hat, watches the young bull rider with cool control. "He gonna make it, son?" he asks Daryl, already knowing the answer.

"I don't know, maybe," Daryl murmurs. "He looks good enough…"

The big brown Brahma bull surges sharply left, then twists hard right…five seconds…six seconds… The young rider on his back does everything he can to hang on tight…seven seconds…until he doesn't. His seat slips, *buzzer sounds*, eight seconds, he's airborne—

The young bull rider flies off the bull's back and slams hard into the thick arena dirt like dead weight, the Brahman bull isn't done with him yet, and he turns back toward the disposed rider.

A bullfighter, early thirties, experienced, dressed like a rodeo clown with painted face, rags over his shirt, and football cleats, moves across the arena, dodging as close as he can in front of the big beast. He touches the bull's head near the deadly horns; Daryl's face lights up, he's impressed and a bit surprised.

The Brahman bull tries to gore the bullfighter, who quickly dashes aside, the big bull now winded, snorting hard, kicks again and turns away. Daryl watches in complete awe as the brown Brahman bull trots toward the open exit gate leading to the livestock chutes, pursued by two pickup men on horseback, both eagerly escorting the monster of a bull out of the warm arena.

The rodeo announcer watches the performance and gives the audience and the young bull rider what they want to hear. "Eight seconds, he made it!" Losing his seat at the end may have cost the young rider some points…

He looks toward the scoreboard across the arena and then at the judges on the ground with their scorecards. The announcer sees the final score. "Seventy-nine points, not a bad ride on that monster!" The young bull rider is excited, he raises his fist in the air, happy to have scored.

Cal calmly exhales, glancing down at Daryl. "Nice call. Guess I'll have to beat that score."

Daryl grins but doesn't answer back. He's still watching the bullfighter, a bit mesmerized. His older brother, Tommy, age thirteen, sharp-eyed, tall and thin with a black cowboy hat, approaches them both with a bag of cotton candy. An attractive brunette, Audrey, age thirty-five, the boy's mother, is walking with him. She stands next to Cal, her husband. Audrey has beautiful features, with a well-defined body in tight jeans and a snug fitting blouse partially unbuttoned on top. She wears a pretty cowboy hat with a silver band around the rim, the cover sitting over her long brown hair. She's the kind of cowgirl that stops roughnecks right in their tracks. Audrey is a former rodeo queen.

"Bet you wish you could ride like that?" Tommy says, handing a fistful of cotton candy to Daryl.

"Maybe, I will, someday..." Daryl replies almost certain and smiles, he grabs the sweet treat from Tommy, stuffing it all in his mouth. He watches the bullfighter as Audrey slides between the boys.

"We only need one bull rider in this family," she says, and leans toward Cal, kissing him. He looks at her a moment longer, and eagerly kisses her back, completely in love.

Another bull rider in the contestant area, Marvin, about age thirty, tough and lean, walks past the family.

Marvin slaps Cal across the shoulder. "Give 'em hell, Cal, you're one of the best!" Extending his open hand.

Cal returns the firm grip. "Damn right I am." He grins and shakes Marvin's hand, then releases his grip.

"Would you mind taking a photo?" Audrey turns toward the bull rider and hands him a small camera with a short strap attached. Marvin takes the camera and raises the lens, waiting a moment for everyone to settle together, and then snaps a photo of the family. Click, flash—time is frozen in place. He hands the camera back to Audrey, admiring her beauty.

"See ya out there, Cal." He grins, turns and keeps moving away.

Cal leans down and scoops up both boys in his arms. "One more bull ride today and we're off to Las Vegas! Either one of you boys ever been there?" He wiggles them both around in his arms. The boys giggle and shake, enjoying the lift, both nodding their heads negatively, they haven't been to the National Finals Rodeo. Cal already knows this, he's just teasing them. He grins and drops the two boys back onto their feet. "Well, you're both are old enough to go now. Whatta say, Momma?" He turns back toward Audrey, kissing her again and holding it close for a moment. "I'm really a lucky man, you know that?" He watches her, Audrey warmly smiles back. She likes his kisses.

"Be careful out there, Daddy," Daryl lightly offers.

Cal laughs and pulls a silver necklace with a small, jeweled cross, from around his neck, placing it over Daryl's head and around his shoulders. The necklace and cross are a bit worn from years of service on Cal's red neck. "Take care of this for me, will ya. It's supposed to bring you luck."

"Don't you need it?" Daryl is a little confused. He looks at his father.

"Nope. I've got all the luck I need right here." Cal smiles at Audrey again, hugging her tight, and he pushes Daryl's hat around on his head. The rodeo announcer's voice thunders across the arena.

", Alright, next up, one of our best riders. He's a four-time Texas State Champion, two-time all-around Tough Guy Finalist…and now looking for his third trip to the National Finals Rodeo in Las Vegas, Cal Weathers!" The crowd roars to life again. The announcer adding more information: "Cal is riding Monster Mascot, one of our toughest bulls in chute three!"

The crowd is shouting louder, clapping, and cheering. Cal smiles one more time at Audrey, turning and moving toward the bucking chutes. He reaches his ride, inside stands a large black-spotted bull with huge wide horns. The animal is impatiently waiting, digging into the dirt, the beast is big and mean, his horns look like wrecking bars. Cal steps over the chute fence rail and eases himself down on the big bull, settling on top of him. The crowd is still cheering as Cal wraps his hand in the bull rope and takes a calm, deep breath, clearing the air of everything else. The black-spotted bull underneath is growing angrier by the second, stomping and kicking in the chute, lurching around—the monster suddenly tries to jump out of the chute and over the gate! Cal hanging on tight, sitting forward and kicking the bull hard in the sides, the bull drops back into the bucking chute. The rough stock crew tightens the rear flank strap around the bull's back end. Cal is ready to make this a great ride.

The crowd starts chanting together in unison: "Ride that bull! Ride that bull!" Daryl, Tommy, and Audrey are watching apprehensively on the other side of the fence. The chute boss shouts toward Cal, "Ready?!"

Cal glances at the bull one more time—and then nods.

Gate bursts open!

Angry massive black-spotted bull shoots straight for the sky and launches out fast! A full-body earthquake on hooves. He comes down twisting and turning, bucking hard. Cal is sticking tight on top of him, riding him clean, balanced, firm and fluid. Three seconds...four seconds...five seconds...the big bull slams forward onto his two front hooves. Cal is digging his heels tighter into the massive beast...

The bull quickly spins into two full circles! A deadly wreck starts to appear on four hooves. Cal is slammed hard forward, his chest hitting the bull's big hump over his shoulders, he slightly loses his seat, he's trying to stay on top, to gain his balance.

The giant beast now starts swinging its horns crazily around over its shoulders, trying to gore Cal and throw him off. Daryl is watching wide-eyed, stunned, and amazed—he's terrified. Audrey is looking completely concerned trying to hold her composure. Tommy is literally shaking in fear.

Six seconds...seven seconds...Cal reseats himself on top taking charge of the beast again!

Eight seconds and the ride buzzer wails across the arena! The crowd explodes into wild cheers and screams. They have just witnessed an incredible ninety-plus point ride with a true Texas bull riding champion! One of their favorite bull riders!

Cal is still on top of the bull, he can't jump off the angry massive beast. It's still bucking and swirling around trying to dislodge him. Cal's hand is stuck inside the bull rope; he can't clear it free. He's desperately trying to work his hand loose. The crowd is seeing the wreck about to happen, now shouting out loud cries of concern and sudden fear. The three rodeo clown bullfighters in the arena are trying to get the bull's attention and help unstrap the bull rope.

Suddenly, the massive bull swirls right and jumps high into the air again, now crashing backward against the metal fence railing! Cal slams hard behind the bull against the iron fence pinned underneath the massive beast. Audrey screams in shock. Tommy grabs the fence, terrified. Daryl doesn't move. He's frozen in place, staring right through the fence slats.

The bullfighters are at the wreck trying to get the bull's attention and get him off Cal. The spotted black bull is swinging its head around, slashing at the rodeo clowns, then suddenly drives one of his horns straight through Cal's upper leg! Ripping flesh and crushing bone!

Cal's riding hand finally comes free; he shouts at the deadly beast in sheer pain. The scream rips from him, raw and inhuman. Cal is trying to stand up and get away from the monster, but he can't stand, his leg is mutilated. Audrey and the boys are watching horrified.

The crowd is shouting for the bullfighters and two pickup men to get the bull off Cal. The pickup men on horseback throw their lariats around the bull's wide head, trying to yank him away from Cal. The bullfighters are slapping the angry beast, engaging him, trying to pull Cal to freedom.

The massive spotted black bull isn't done.

He slams his giant skull backward against Cal's face! Breaking Cal's nose and knocking him out. Blood gushes out everywhere. Audrey is crying in desperation; she wants to run into the arena. Her husband is being mangled to death. The giant beast finally stands on his four hooves and shakes out his bloody horn. Cal is unmoving, lying in the dirt inside a growing pool of blood. The pickup men are yanking on the bull trying to pull him toward the arena exit gate.

Paramedics rush in, trying to get close to Cal. Daryl grips the fence tighter, his head right between the metal slats. He stares at the giant bull—who spins around and sees Daryl looking at him!

The massive bull looks right at Daryl; it suddenly snorts loudly and charges toward the small boy, jerking the two pickup men's ropes loose from their hands and saddle horns on horseback. Everyone is startled, there's loud screams of shock and sudden silence in the open stadium seats.

The giant black bull charges across the arena toward Daryl! Sliding to a sudden stop on all four hooves right in front of him. The massive beast bellows and blows hot breath onto Daryl's face, blowing his hair back under his cowboy hat and covering Daryl's face in thick, wet spittle. The bull bellows again a second time, defiant, deadly, a real man-killer. Daryl stares back at the monster beast. Unmoving, he doesn't flinch.

Audrey is frozen in shock. Tommy can't believe what he just saw. Tears swelling in his eyes.

The pickup men ride up and finally herd the bull away. Its nostrils flare one more time, it bellows loudly again at Daryl, stomping its hooves into the ground, then it's gone. The pickup men herding the deadly animal toward the livestock arena gate.

Audrey squeezes Daryl's arm with genuine concern, then quickly slips between the slats of the arena fence, squeezing through and running through the thick dirt

toward Cal. He's still lying unconscious on the arena
floor. The paramedics are wrapping his leg in splints.
Tommy is crying next to Daryl, terrified.

Daryl's fingers squeeze the cross around his neck.

He looks at his father lying hurt.

Unmoving. Bleeding in the dirt.

But he doesn't cry...

2

BULL RIDER

PRESENT DAY—PECOS, TEXAS

Twenty-eight years later...

Same kind of chute gate. Same kind of thick dirt. Same kind of angry bulls.

But this time, a grown-up Daryl Weathers, now age thirty-six, his face aged more, but still young looking, is the one straddling the black beast of anger and fury. Older, stronger and tougher, the silver necklace and jeweled cross his father gave him still hangs around his neck and lies against his chest. The lucky charm dulled a little more from another two and half decades of visible service.

Daryl touches the little cross. Not so much for luck, but for the same habit of genuine honor and respect he has for his injured father, whom he rarely talks to anymore. The black Charolais bull underneath him is a smaller compact aggressive Mexican bull that shudders and stomps in the dirt, the feisty animal eager to get out of the chute gate.

Daryl smashes his brown cowboy hat down over his eyebrows, gripping with one hand the tight bull rope wrapped around the animal's muscled back. He's been riding bulls of all breeds for over eighteen years now. He lets the bull settle a moment then nods at the gate man.

The chute gate flies open! The bull exploding like a ball of mixed fury—spinning, lunging, kicking, jerking hard right into a full circle, then back to the left in a semi-circle. The Charolais breed is smaller and quicker than the old-style larger bulls. Daryl hangs on tight, his muscle fiber locked into place, his riding arm extended in front of his body, his boot heels planted firmly around the bull.

Three seconds…four seconds…five seconds…the ride looks good…now the feisty bull is jerking and spinning harder to the right, then does another sharp turn back to the left. Six seconds…Daryl begins to lose his seat, his grip is coming undone inside the rope…seven seconds, he's slipping further off the bull—

Daryl is abruptly thrown off the bull's back and hits the arena floor hard, his hat dislodged and tossed aside, he does a full face plant into the thick dirt. The eight-second buzzer sounds loudly as now a big zero flashes on the scoreboard over the large crowd. Several groan collectively, shaking their heads in disappointment. They expected a better ride from Daryl, who is still lying face first in the heavy arena dirt. Daryl pulls his head from the muck and raises himself onto his knees, staring at the big zero on the overhead scoreboard. His face is covered in dark dirt, he spits out some of the filth onto the arena floor, watching the Mexican bull trotting around the other side of the arena. Its work is done;

there's no further interest in the knocked-off cowboy. The two pickup men on horseback easily move the animal toward the livestock exit gate on the arena floor.

Daryl angrily grabs a handful of dirt and flings it away from him in disgust. He should have ridden this simple bull. He's been on dozens of bulls like this one before, but he didn't have his head in the game today. The two pickup men push the Mexican bull into the arena exit gate and turn around, riding back past Daryl toward their starting spots under the announcer's booth. Dust scatters and settles again around Daryl still sitting in the dirt, followed closely by his pride as he swallows hard.

One of the painted rodeo clowns brings Daryl his hat. "What the hell was that all about?" he asks. He knows Daryl should have ridden the beast.

"He turned sharp—into my left," Daryl mutters quietly, knowing it's a lame excuse.

"Looks like you gave up, dude." The rodeo clown hands him his hat and watches him for a moment as Daryl stands and grabs the smashed-in hat. He punches the middle crown back out and turns toward the rodeo performer's gate, walking through the thick dirt under polite applause from the crowd in the grandstands sitting above the railing, and exits the arena floor.

Daryl grabs his bull strap hanging on the fence dropped there by one of the pickup men when they rode past. He throws the riding strap over his shoulder and walks toward his bag full of rodeo gear, dropping the bull rope inside and starts unbuckling his riding chinks.

Rory Dean, age thirty-two, a good friend, part Hispanic with classic cowboy features and well-muscled shoulders, steps toward Daryl. He stares a few beats at him before giving him crap. "You should have rode that one. He's no different than the others." Daryl pulls his chinks off, looking at Rory. He doesn't offer an immediate response, just watching him. "Why didn't you stick to him, you were at seven seconds?" Rory isn't being politically polite and doesn't pretend to know the answer. "You're not going to make the circuit finals riding like that, amigo." He shakes his head.

Daryl lays his chinks on top of his riding rope, he pulls a half-empty pint of whiskey from the rodeo bag, taking a big swig of the calming amber liquid. He offers the open flask to Rory, looking at him a little closer. "Don't you got someone else to complain to?" Daryl holds the whiskey in front of Rory.

"Maybe you ought to try this sport with less whiskey before you ride." Rory grabs the flask and takes a short swig, handing the whiskey back to Daryl.

"I don't remember asking for your advice?" Daryl takes another drink and looks at Rory again, who shakes his head a bit disappointed. Two younger bull riders in their early twenties walk past them, the first one larger than the second rider, they both wear big smiles.

"Keep up the good work, Weathers. We like it when you set us up for easy cash." The first bull rider laughs loudly and looks at the second bull rider, he playfully punches his riding partner in the shoulder, they laugh together. The second bull rider pretending the punch in the shoulder hurts. "Ohh, oouucchh...he bucked me off..." almost a low wail and cry. He grins and they both laugh together again, turning away now and walking toward the riding chutes. Daryl wants to slap them both.

He and Rory watch them depart. Rory shakes his head and looks at Daryl, giving an honest assessment. "Why are you still doing this, Daryl? You're gonna be thirty-seven in about two months. It's time to think about retiring, don't ya think?" He watches Daryl another couple of moments, who pushes down his chinks and riding rope deeper into his bull gear bag, zipping it closed.

He looks at Rory. "You're thirty-one, and think you got all the answers, don't you?" He stares at Rory. "I can still compete with the youngsters." He hefts the bull riding bag over his shoulder. The half-empty whiskey flask is still in one hand. Daryl isn't buying any doubt right now.

Rory looks at him, shaking his head. "Quit riding bulls and go work for your daddy on the ranch. He could use your help raising cattle, you know that. That'd be a hell of a lot easier than getting yourself beat up like this every week." Daryl watches him closer; he lifts the whiskey flask one more time.

"My daddy offering me a job?" Daryl stares at him and takes another swig from the flask. He starts to move away.

"I'm just saying it would be a lot safer. I'm offering you reality, damn it. You're just in this for the easy cowgirls and the hard drinking. You need to move past all that. You could have been a champion. But that's over, we both know it." Rory is making an honest statement, as Daryl looks straight at him. He likes Rory, they've been good friends for many years, they've traveled the rodeo circuit together for a long time, Daryl taught him how to ride bulls. Daryl doesn't want to hear it right now.

"Let's go find a barstool."

"What? I still gotta ride."

"Then loan me twenty bucks, and I'll see you in a while."

"You still owe me five hundred dollars! Why would I

give you another twenty to throw away?" Rory is a little ruffled now. Daryl sticks his hand out, another common practice. Rory stares at him for a moment, not at all amused. He begrudgingly digs into the front pocket of his loose-fitting jeans for some cash. He pulls out a couple twenty spots and peels one off, handing it to Daryl, who quickly swipes it from him.

"Put it on my tab."

"Yeah, you're welcome, partner." Rory shakes his head, not the least surprised, but he can't help but love Daryl, a strong friend for over ten years. Daryl turns and starts walking toward the exit gate. "Stay out of trouble!" Rory throws the words across the contestant area at Daryl.

Who doesn't look back.

———

STREETLIGHTS BOUNCE OFF THE NIGHTTIME EXTERIOR OF an older run-down single-story motel containing about sixteen outdated and well-used motel rooms. All the beat-up doors are at ground level facing the open parking lot with about half a dozen cowboy trucks parked outside.

Inside one of the motel rooms, which smells of sweet perfume mixed with sweat and fresh whiskey, Daryl rolls off a pretty cowgirl, Jenna, age twenty-eight, with good tan lines, tight curves and nice breasts. He slides onto his back, catching his breath and quickly reaching to his right for the open whiskey bottle sitting on the nightstand beside him. He takes a long slow swig and props the bottle on his chest staring at the ceiling, thinking about his bad bull ride.

Jenna lies beside him, trying to get more comfortable

and snuggling up with him. Daryl isn't the snuggling kind and he slides away from her a little further toward his edge of the bed. He offers her the open whiskey bottle. "Thirsty?"

Jenna raises her head and looks at Daryl, then the open bottle. She knows they already had enough to drink, one of the reasons she went to bed with him so quickly. Her expression changes slightly from passion to obvious irritation.

"Are you serious?" She tries to lay her head back down on his chest. Daryl slides further away, partially off the bed and sits up against the rickety headboard, taking another drink from the almost empty whiskey bottle. Jenna looks disappointed. She doesn't understand why he's acting this way now. "What's wrong? Why are you moving away from me now? I thought we just had a great time together?" She touches his chest, rubbing her hand through some of the chest hairs.

Daryl is more enamored with the whiskey bottle than the beautiful young lady lying naked in bed with him. "I-I'm sorry, it's not you. I just got a lot of things on my mind is all." He sets the nearly empty whiskey bottle back on the nightstand. He doesn't get closer to her. Jenna is hurt.

"Obviously, I'm no longer one of those things on your mind right now, am I?" Jenna is feeling a little taken advantage of. She rolls away from him and reaches for her pack of cigarettes lying on top of the scratched-up nightstand on her side of the bed. She slides up into a sitting position like Daryl, covering her breasts with the thin sheet and lights a cigarette. She inhales a deep puff, then exhales a wide cloud of smoke engulfing the room. "Maybe you should just leave?" She really doesn't understand why he's acting this way.

"I'm sorry, I didn't mean it like that." Daryl glances at her, she really is pretty. He looks across the room again, still not getting closer to her, or letting her know how much he appreciated their time together.

Jenna takes another hit from her cigarette; she exhales more smoke and looks over at him. "Are you always like this with all the cowgirls you take to bed?" She stares at him, watching him closer and waits a moment. "You know, the first time I saw you ride bulls in Amarillo…I thought, there's a real cowboy with a great future. A cowboy that's going to go places, just like his daddy did."

Daryl quickly glances at her. His mood is changing now. It's all about his father again. He leans toward her. "Don't talk about my daddy. You don't know the first thing about him."

Jenna stares at him for a moment, holding her lit cigarette between her fingers. His sudden change in attitude makes her feel taken advantage of and slightly abused. "You're a real dumbass bastard, you know that?" She smashes out the cigarette in the partially filled ashtray on the nightstand and slips out of bed, grabbing her rodeo clothes and covering herself. She walks around to his side of the bed toward the door. "I thought you were honest and a nice guy?"

Daryl sits up on the edge of the bed and grabs his button-up shirt from the floor, slipping the rodeo printed fabric over his head, he grabs his underwear and pants off the floor, sliding his feet through the legs and standing, he pulls the garments up to his waist and buckles his big rodeo belt tight. He steps into his cowboy boots, glancing toward her. "Hey, thanks for a good time. Sorry it turned out this way."

Jenna stares at him, she's bitter now. She can't believe

he's turned out like this against her. "Don't flatter your-self, asshole. You should leave."

"It wasn't flattery…" He stands in front of her, closer now. "There's plenty of pretty cowgirls wanting to sleep with bull riders." Jenna raises her hand to slap him in the face. Daryl quickly grabs her hand. He's been here before. "You were one of the best I had in a while. If that makes you feel any better?" Jenna is staring at him, uncertain what to say now. "I mean that. Thank you for a great time. Let me know if you want to get together again." He moves past her and starts to the door, grab-bing the door handle. He stands there for a moment with his back turned away, as if he suddenly realizes he was really being stupid and should apologize to Jenna and spend the rest of the night with this beautiful woman.

The almost empty whiskey bottle smashes hard against the doorframe next to him! The glass bottle shat-ters into several pieces, spraying him with golden whiskey.

"Get the hell out!" Jenna shouts from behind him.

She is standing there hurt, one arm covering her nakedness. Daryl turns around and looks at her for another moment. He's got whiskey spilled on his face and cowboy shirt. He looks at her for another couple of seconds, then opens the door and exits, the broken whiskey bottle crunching under his cowboy boots.

He shuts the door behind him.

———

A MODEST CAFÉ EARLY THE NEXT MORNING WHERE DARYL and Rory sit across from each other at a booth eating a breakfast of scrambled eggs and ham. Several other customers are sitting throughout the café eating their morning hotcakes, biscuits, sausage, bacon, and eggs.

An attractive waitress, late thirties, slim and cute, comes over to the table and refills Daryl and Roy's coffee cups. Daryl immediately notices her partially opened blouse, her tight breasts sitting nice and firm inside her snug top. The waitress smiles at the bull rider and turns away. Rory notices Daryl is watching the waitress from behind. "You didn't get enough action last night?" He cuts a chunk of his ham steak, mixing it with his over-easy eggs, and takes another bite.

Daryl, who looks a little tired and partially hungover from the night before, his eyes a little red, sips on his fresh cup of black coffee, still watching the cute waitress helping other patrons. "Ya know, I was thinking that we could drive up to Wichita Falls for one day, then over to Lawton after that. We could do two rodeos in one quick trip."

"You wanna go up to Oklahoma?" Rory looks over at him.

"It's a good option. They pay well." Daryl sets his coffee cup down, digging into his own breakfast, scooping up a bite of scrambled eggs.

"They don't pay for crap there. We should go to San Angelo, it's closer to home and the purse is a lot bigger." Rory watches him and shovels another forkful of breakfast into his mouth.

Daryl shrugs his shoulders. He looks back at the cute waitress and she smiles at him. He smiles back, enjoying her nice breasts and her pretty face. The waitress turns away.

"You know, San Angelo qualifies for the circuit finals," Rory gobbles down some more food. "You should get yerself focused again on winning and earning some money."

Daryl digs into his plate, swallowing a large helping of gold and white eggs, he swipes his chin clean. "San Angelo is a tough lineup...all the younger riders are going to be down there."

"You mean Rex Winslow is going to be down there?" Rory takes another bite of his breakfast and stares at Daryl, who is now glaring back at him.

"Rex means nothing to me." Daryl tries to ignore the familiar name.

"Yeah, right...Rex wants to beat you more than anyone else sitting on a pair of bull horns. Ever since you tried to date his older sister." Rory grins now, a bit amused.

Daryl looks back at him. Rory has his attention. "Okay, I'll admit, she's pretty hot and I was a bit infatuated with her. But that was last year and you know I'm not looking for a permanent fix. Not right now, anyway." He throws a slight grin at Rory and digs back in for some more food. He glances toward the cute waitress again, she's leaning over, wiping down a table just a couple booths over, firm breasts sweeping low over the front of her arms. Daryl likes the view.

"Rex's sister was married, wasn't she?" Rory teases some more.

Daryl looks at him. "She's divorced." He starts thinking about Rex's sister and glances back at Rory for a moment. "Speaking of married women, did Sarah Jane call you this morning?" He throws some teasing back into Rory's face.

"Leave my wife out of this." Rory isn't amused now. His expression grows a bit more serious.

Daryl keeps the teasing going. "Waaa, waaa, waaa...no

phone sex makes Rory a dull, little boy." He's enjoying the slap back on Rory. A common occurrence they share with each other all the time.

"Shut up already, okay?" Rory looks slightly upset; he doesn't like the conversation now. Daryl's cell phone suddenly buzzes—he glances at the screen.

"Are you kidding me...?" It's his father's telephone number with the name CAL in big bold black letters spread across his phone screen. Daryl doesn't want to answer the call.

Rory sees the name on the screen. He suddenly smiles and throws more dirt back at Daryl. "Daddy still checking on you, little man?" Grinning now, Daryl is shaking his head. He looks over at Rory, then turns away and answers the phone call. "Ya, hello?" Glancing outside the café window.

"That's one heck of a way to greet your father..." Cal with his ear stuck to his cell phone stands next to a handsome dun horse gelding. "I know you have my phone number, son. Why haven't you called me in the past couple of weeks?" The double sliding doors to a large horse barn entrance are slid open just behind Cal and the dun horse. In his late sixties now, Cal still looks trim and in decent shape, but he sadly moves with a noticeable limp. Compliments of the bad leg injury he received from the deadly bull who ripped his flesh open and smashed his bones many years earlier. Cal brushes down the dun colored horse, stepping on his good leg as best as possible to ease the discomfort. "Word floated down this way that you're just east of us here near Pecos. You comin' to visit or not?" He swipes the dun's thick coat, moving the brush across the horse's strong shoulders.

Daryl is sitting in the café booth looking at Rory

now. He pauses a moment before replying, staring at Rory. "We're thinking of going up to Wichita Falls for a couple days. Then maybe Lawton. They're both good rodeos with some good prize money."

"You're going to Oklahoma?" There's a quiet moment on the phone, while Cal brushes the dun. "I'm sure Rory would rather see that pretty wife of his and his two little girls, than your rough face for another ten days." Cal swipes under the belly of the dun horse clearing off the loose hair. "What's Rory say about Lawton?" He bends down to get under the horse a little closer, causing him pain in his bad leg.

Daryl waits another moment, looking straight at Rory. "He's good with Lawton." Daryl is nodding at Rory, who is shaking his head no—he doesn't want to go there.

Cal swipes the back end of the dun horse and tosses the grooming brush down into a nearby basket. "Son, you're less than two hundred miles from home. Get your butt down here to the ranch and see me and your brother...I know you're probably hurting for money... you always are..."

Daryl is still watching Rory; he grimaces at Cal's comment. They have had this conversation a hundred times before. Rory is still shaking his head no. He stares over the table at Daryl, he's serious and doesn't want to go north. Daryl has a natural talent for riding bulls like his father did and can ride anything underneath him, but he's always broke when traveling on the road, because he plays around and drinks too much. Rory almost always pays for everything, including the fuel and hotel rooms. It's easier for Daryl to play being a bull rider and to chase the pretty cowgirls and drink heavy every night, than actually take the sport seriously. Besides, he doesn't like to compete for big prize money, which drives Rory crazy. Part of the hurt Daryl still carries inside from watching his father's almost mortal bull wreck. He likes to ride bulls, but his heart isn't into being a champion.

"Let me talk it over with Rory." Daryl looks at his good friend, who is shaking his head, as a way of saying let's go home.

"Why you gotta ask Rory? Are you two dating now or something?" Cal is playing him and throwing it back in Daryl's face, who looks at Rory and can see that he's ready to see his wife and daughters for a couple days.

"How's Tommy doing?" Daryl leans back in the booth at the table.

Cal still has the cell phone stuffed under his chin as he throws a colorful Indian blanket and ranch saddle on top of the dun-colored horse, pulling the cinch tight underneath. The pain in his damaged leg grabbing him again when he steps around the animal. He picks up the horse's bridle and reins, placing the tack over the Dun's head and ears, and slipping the curved bit into the horse's mouth. The horse easily accepts the bit and chomps on it a moment.

"Tommy is doing just fine. Get yerself down here. I'll throw some steaks on the grill for dinner tonight." He sets the reins over the dun horse's neck and clicks off the phone, stuffing the device in his cowboy vest pocket. Then steps with his good leg into the stirrup.

Daryl hears the phone click off; he glances at the blank screen, then back at Rory, who is ready to give him crap again. "Daddy tellin' ya to get yer broke ass home?" he teases Daryl some more.

"I don't want to hear it." Daryl isn't amused. He sips the last of his coffee, looking across the café toward the pretty waitress.

Rory shakes his head and slides out of the booth. He

stands up, pulling some cash from his front pants pocket, he throws a few bills on the table with a nice tip for the pretty waitress.

"That tip is for the waitress, not you." Rory looks at Daryl, like he might take it. "I'll get the truck. Let's go home for a couple days." He turns and starts walking toward the front door, then stops and looks back at Daryl, making sure the money is still on the table. He grins and exits out the front door.

Daryl watches him leave the café and walk into the parking lot toward his truck.

He looks back at the blank screen on his cell phone.

Turns it off.

3
THE RANCH

Rory's big Dodge dually truck, with his gooseneck trailer hitch attached in the bed, drives along the narrow gravel road toward the large ranch house sitting under some shaded trees. The afternoon sun is starting to drop toward the western horizon. Daryl sits in the front passenger seat, looking at the open barbed-wire fenced pastures filled with tall Texas prairie grass, strong looking horses, and beef cattle as they drive past. The truck pulls up to the ranch house and stops.

Daryl steps out through the passenger door and grabs his rodeo bag and suitcase with rollers on the bottom from the back seat of the truck. Rory watches him from the front driver's seat. Daryl stands outside the open truck doors; he shuts the back door and glances back into the cab through the front door. "See ya in a couple days."

"Sounds good, amigo." Rory waves adios as Daryl slams the front truck door closed and watches his traveling partner pull the truck away. Big brother, Tommy, aged forty now, tall and muscled and thin, all grown up like Daryl, comes toward his little brother from the horse barn. He walks right up to Daryl, just barely just inches from his face. His expression looks harsh.

"Hey, dumbass!"

"Hey, jackass!"

Daryl throws it right back and looks at Tommy for a moment, then grabs his older brother, the two embracing each other and laughing together. Tommy scoops up Daryl's rodeo bag.

"Daddy said you wuz comin' home for a few days. It's been almost two months since we saw you. How ya been doin' on the circuit? Winning anything?"

Daryl picks up his suitcase. "Not much, there's a lot of tough competitors out there nowadays." He looks around the ranch, actually feeling a little happy to be back for a short visit. "How's Daddy doing, anyway?" They start toward the front porch of the ranch house. Tommy reaches the steps first and starts up the stairs with a wide handle on one side.

"He's doing okay…most days. Never stops working of course. Wish that he would slow down a bit, his bad leg is giving him more grief now." Daryl follows him up the steps. "He still rides the Dun horse almost every day around the ranch. So, I guess that's a good thing."

They stand at the top of the stairs. Tommy turns around. "I worry about his heart now." Standing under the white painted roof with one by six sheets covering the pretty wide porch. There's a porch swing and couple of wood chairs on the other end.

"His heart? What's that all about?" Daryl didn't expect to hear that.

"He's been having some pain in his chest recently. Thinks it might have something to do with his bad leg."

Tommy watches Daryl, studying his face. "I've tried to get him to go to the doctor."

Daryl stares at him. He has his own thoughts about their father. "Being angry at everyone all the time might have something to do with it?" Daryl is straightforward about how he feels.

Tommy looks at his brother. "You're the only one he's mad at all the time, Daryl." Watching his little brother another moment. "Wish you would stop making him so upset."

Daryle watches Tommy. "You're jest jealous."

"Of course, I am...dumbass." Tommy grins. "Then again, we all can't be drinking every day and chasing pretty tail all the time like it's part of their job." Tommy is teasing him now.

Daryl grins, more laughter is exchanged between the two brothers.

"We start branding in a couple weeks...I really could use your help." Tommy is hoping Daryl will step up and stay at the ranch for a while, but he already knows what his brother is probably thinking.

"Wish I could, but I'll be in San Angelo next week." Daryl is looking at him.

"That's a big one, huh? Circuit qualifier?" Tommy knows it's a good rodeo.

"Yep, then on to the National Finals." Daryl looks at him closer. "Of course, you already know that it's a big rodeo, don't you?" Tommy nods his head, of course he does. They smile together again.

The front screen door swings wide open. Cal walks out onto the porch, the pain in his bad leg is a bit obvious. He stands there for a moment looking at his two sons, then moves toward Daryl and hugs him. "Well, I see you can still find the place," slapping him over the shoulder. "You hungry?"

"Heck yes, if you're cooking." Daryl puts his arm around his father. They turn around and start toward the screen door of the ranch house. Tommy likes to see them together.

"Thanks for making it home to see us, son." Cal squeezes Daryl once again, as they walk through the front screen door. Tommy follows with a smile still stuck on his face.

———

CAL, DARYL, AND TOMMY SIT AT A WIDE OUTDOOR TABLE surrounded by large comfortable chairs centered on the cement patio off the back of the ranch house. Three empty meal plates with dirty knives, steak bones, forks, and napkins sit on the table in front of them.

Daryl is exaggerating about a recent bull ride.

"So that big-sons-of-a-buck tries to pitch me left, then right, then did this little crow hop and bucked back up again…" He's laughing now, Cal and Tommy are grinning. "I dug a little deeper into his sides and rode him around the arena like I owned him…"

Tommy laughs, Cal doesn't look that impressed now. "How many bulls you actually ride in the past two months?" His stare fixed on Daryl.

"What do you mean?"

"How many have you actually stayed on and scored?"

Daryl shifts, a bit uncomfortable. "I dunno, maybe fifteen…or twenty?

"Twenty bulls and you don't have anything to show for it?" Cal isn't buying his bragging.

"Well, I've had a few broken bull ropes and a couple

flank cinches that came loose." He grins at Tommy, shaking his head. Daryl picks up his whiskey glass off the patio table and guzzles the remainder. "Here's to the Rodeo Man," toasting the two others. Cal isn't buying it.

"You've been riding bulls for almost eighteen years now. Isn't that right?"

"Yeah, just about that long."

"And you still got nuthin' to show for it."

Daryl stares at his father, he's ready for another drink. "Do we gotta do this again?"

"I always played by the rules." Cal is pressing him. "Married a good woman and raised two boys. That's what the cowboy life is all about."

"We all know you got cheated out of the National Championships." Daryl looks him straight in the face. "But it wasn't my fault."

Cal stares at him and slides his plate away. "You've got the most natural talent I've ever seen for a bull rider. And all you ever done is piss it away. Chasing girls and drinking like a fool. You could have been a champion. One of the best bull riders ever."

"C'mon, Daddy." Daryl doesn't want to go down this road again.

"It's time to stop riding and start working for a living. You never wanted the world title anyway, so I don't see any reason for you to keep this charade going? We need help here on the ranch. Your brother works hard seven days a week to keep this place going."

Daryl shifts uneasy, he really wants another drink. He stares at Cal waiting for the next words. Tommy lifts himself from his chair and stands. "Who wants dessert?"

"I'll take another drink." Daryl is still staring at Cal.

"You drink too much." Cal is straightforward and serious.

Daryl waits a moment. "Yeah, and that's comin' from the one person that ran our mother off because he started drinking like a fish." Cal stares at him. Daryl has hit a deep nerve.

"I was always there for her. I started drinking after I got hurt. You know that."

"You weren't there for her at the end. We <u>all</u> know that." Daryl is bringing an ugly part of their lives back to the present. Cal doesn't want to hear it.

"I was as close as a cowboy can get to going to Las Vegas! To the National Championships! But you…you've never wanted to be a champion! To be a real winner!" Cal's face is flush now. "You just keep throwing it all away!"

"I'm not doing it for you!" Daryl's face is red now also; he's staring Cal back down. Tommy doesn't like the after-dinner show.

"Damn right, you're not doing it for me!" Cal glares back at Daryl. They've been down this road too many times before. "I loved your mother. There's never was or has been anyone else."

"She died before she was forty-two!"

Tommy grabs Daryl's empty plate, weary of the exchange. "C'mon, guys."

Cal is upset at Daryl. "Why can't you be more like Tommy? Work a real job for a living?"

"Here we go…" Tommy starts scooping up the other empty plates.

"Tommy can't ride bulls!" Daryl is still staring at Cal.

Tommy stops for a moment and looks down at Daryl. Cal stares at him as well. Tommy stacks their plates in his hands. "I've never rode bulls and never will. You're the only one left in the family that can ride bulls, Daryl." Tommy holds the three empty plates in one hand. Cal's eyes are set on Daryl, his face still flushed, yet there seems to be a sadness in Cal's eyes.

"Why is it, you can't just let me be myself?" Daryl looks at Cal. "What I want to do, not what you want me to do?" Tommy steps away and sets the empty meal plates on a nearby outdoor bar countertop. He reaches around the other side for a bottle of Texas whiskey.

Cal is still pushing Daryl. "You've had a chance to be one of the best bull riders in the world. You could have been great." Cal looks upset and disappointed. "You pissed it away."

"I don't want to be great—and I don't want to be the best." Daryl is being honest.

"That's ridiculous. Every good rider wants to be great." Cal stares back at him. Daryl watches.

"Do you want me to leave?" Daryl is staring at Cal, who looks at him now with his teeth clenched, he waits another moment, now calming himself down a little.

"Of course not. This is your home." He stares at Daryl, letting that sit and then decides to change the subject for something better to talk about. "Let's saddle the dun and Buckskin tomorrow morning and go for a ride around the ranch. How's that sound?"

Daryl glances at Tommy walking back over to the table with the whiskey bottle. He's feeling more at home now that the conversation with Cal is over. Family is family. "That'd be great." He offers a genuine smile, as Cal stands. It's hard to keep his balance on the bad leg.

"I've had enough; it was a good dinner." Looking at both his sons. "Good night, boys. Don't drink too much." He looks back at Daryl, he's serious with his words. He turns and starts for the house, glancing back over his shoulder. "See ya both in the morning," as he exits the patio through the double rear glass doors.

Tommy stands at the table and pours Daryl another whiskey. He fills a second glass for himself. "Don't be so hard on him. He still loves you."

"Really? Since that bull wreck when we were kids, it seems like he's always had to take all his worst crap out on me. Why is that?" He picks up his whiskey glass. Rolling the whiskey around inside.

"Cause you're a dummy."

"Shut up, stupid—"

Daryl smiles and clinks his whiskey glass against Tommy's. He leans back and guzzles a large portion of the whiskey in one drink. Tommy shakes his head, watching him down his drink. He lifts his own glass and sips on his whiskey.

The two brothers grinning at each other.

4
PAYCHECK

RODEO ARENA - LLANO, TEXAS

DARYL SITS IN THE BUCKING CHUTE ON A FAT GRAY BULL with one horn bent. He tightens his grip on the bull rope and tugs on his hat. The banner hanging over the bucking chutes says, Llano, Texas—Open Pro Rodeo. The stands are filled with eager rodeo fans cheering all the cowboys and cowgirls competing in the open arena. Daryl rechecks his grip and nods at the gate man. Chute gate swings open.

He's out of the chute!

Gray bull bursts through the gate, he jumps left high off the ground, then turns right, Daryl is stuck on his back, riding him like he wants to win. Five seconds, six seconds, seven seconds... Daryl is deep in his seat... Eight seconds, the buzzer rings loud and Daryl quickly dismounts like it was all fun and easy. The rodeo crowd is cheering and clapping, it looked like a good ride.

Daryl hustles off the arena floor toward the contestant's gate near the bucking chutes, the rodeo clowns and pickup men on horseback moving the gray bull away toward the livestock exit gate on the other end of the arena. Daryl leaves the arena and goes through the contestant gate; Rory is standing there in his riding chinks. He excitedly high-fives Daryl, slapping him across the shoulder. "Nice ride, Cowboy! San Angelo just got a little closer!"

Daryl unsnaps his leather chinks, waiting for the score overhead, he sticks his cowbell and bull rope into his rodeo bag, grabbing his whiskey flask. The score pops up overhead on the electronic scoreboard—it's a seventy-nine. Good score!

"Second place. That's about fifteen hundred dollars! Not bad for two days of work." Daryl takes a hit from his silver whiskey flask.

"Hell, that's not bad pay for a whole week worth of work." Rory grabs his riding rope and stuffs it into his own riding bag. Daryl offers him a drink, and Rory declines. "No, thanks."

"Where you sittin' at?" Daryl looks at Rory a little closer and starts to take another sip from his whiskey flask, then stops and looks at the silver canteen. He thinks about it a moment, then tightens the cap on the silver flask and shoves the whiskey back into the rodeo bag.

"Fifth or sixth, I'm not sure." Rory is a bit surprised that Daryl only took one drink. "Might work out on the averages, I hope so."

"That'd be great..." Daryl zips up his rodeo bag, "Since I can't keep supporting the both of us on the road forever." He grins at Rory and laughs, jabbing at him for fun.

"You're so full of bullshit." Rory throws it back, also laughing. "I'm the one always paying the bills."

"Heck after today, I might be able to pay you the five hundred dollars I owe you." Daryl grins at Rory.

"That'd be nice." Rory closes his rodeo bag, looking at Daryl with an almost serious expression. "But please don't say it unless you really mean it. I might get teary-eyed." He laughs at Daryl.

Another bull rider, thin and short, releases from the bucking chute gate, Daryl and Rory turn around watching him ride. Three seconds...four seconds...the bull rider is having a tough time staying on the back of the bull...five seconds...the thin bull rider is dumped hard onto the arena floor.

Daryl slaps Rory across the shoulders.

"Let's go get my paycheck." He picks up his rodeo bag. "Then go to the closest bar."

"Give me my five hundred dollars first. I don't want you spending it all at the bar." Rory grabs his bag and follows. "I need to send the money to Sarah Jane and the girls."

"I'll give it to you when we cash my check at the bar."

"Of course you will." Rory slapping him across the shoulders.

Daryl grinning at Rory as they head for the stadium exit.

———

DARYL AND RORY SIT AT A POPULAR LOCAL BAR SIPPING their drinks. It's a younger crowd with lots of attractive cowboys and cowgirls. Rory finishes his beer and slips out of his chair. He stands, looking at Daryl. "Gotta go call home. See ya at the hotel soon..."

He grins and nods at the female bartender, sliding a

couple dollars over the bar top toward her, then knuckle-bumps Daryl and exits the rear of the bar.

Daryl sits there for a moment thinking about his ride today, he glances across the dance floor and sees Christy Holden, age thirty-two, a very pretty, blond cowgirl, enter the bar. She comes through the front door with several rodeo friends. Daryl is a bit surprised to see Christy—this is his bull riding nemesis, Rex Winslow's older sister. The same woman he tried to date about a year ago. Daryl and Rex do not get along well at all. They are always competing aggressively against each other. Rex, who is about age thirty, almost six years younger than Daryl, usually gets the upper hand on the bull riding scores. He's more focused and takes the sport more seriously, which is what every bull rider wants to do. Except Daryl.

Daryl watches pretty Christy and the others for a few moments as they move through the saloon. Now Christy notices him sitting alone at the bar, she offers him a pleasant smile. Christy looks the other away again, talking to her friends and ignoring Daryl. He finishes his whiskey glass and stands at the bar for a moment, then works his way across the crowded floor toward Christy.

One of Christy's best friends, Maria, age twenty-nine, a gorgeous Latina cowgirl with nice felt hat, tight blouse, and colorful boots, is standing next to her. Daryl approaches them and Maria isn't too happy to see him. She immediately lets Daryl know how she feels about his trying to date Christy. "Oh, oh, here comes trouble again." Maria exhales the words firmly at Christy, as Daryl steps toward them.

"What are you doin' here, Christy? I didn't think I'd see you before San Angelo?" Daryl moves close and

Christy is watching him, she likes Daryl. Her brother Rex hates him. Maria steps between them.

"We're actually just leaving." She stands right in front of Christy and looks Daryl straight in the face.

"Well, it's always nice to see you too, Maria." Daryl isn't buying her negative attitude.

He smiles at Christy, who smiles back and responds favorably. "Nice ride today." She's being honest.

"Seriously?" Maria frowns harder. "There's a heck of a lot of better bull riders on this rodeo circuit than this guy."

Daryl looks at Maria again. He wants to tell her to shove it right up her tight butt but he holds back his comments at her. He looks at Christy. "Thanks for the compliment." Staring at her another moment with a warm smile. "So, where's your brother, Rex?"

Now he's teasing her.

"Oh, give me a break!" Maria has her hands on her hips, looking very attractive, but not impressed with Daryl. "You two hate each other, why would you even ask her that?"

Christy has a pleasant look on her face; she smiles again at Daryl. "He already qualified for San Angelo. He'll be there next week." She likes Daryl, regardless of what her brother and friend both think.

"You both wanna drink? I'm buying." Daryl is watching Christy; he grins at Maria.

"A drink from you?! No way! We know where this is going!" Maria isn't kidding around. The two other cowboys and their girlfriends who came inside with Christy and Maria are listening to the heated conversation. One of the bigger cowboys, Donny, steps toward Daryl. He's taller and larger, a bulldogger.

"Why don't you just leave these two girls alone and

vamoose out of here, amigo." Donny is staring right at Daryl, ready for trouble. Daryl sizes up the larger bull-dogger. He looks back at Christy.

"I heard your divorce is final."

Donny steps closer. "Hey now, that's not very cool." Daryl stares the bulldogger straight in the face.

"What's wrong with askin' a simple question? Just trying to get my facts straight is all."

The larger cowboy steps closer to Daryl, clenching his fists, his face tight and taunt. Christy puts her hand out and stops him. "It's okay, Donny. We know each other." Her friend looks at her questionable, then looks back at Daryl. He moves back one step. Christy looks at Daryl. "I'll let my brother Rex know you were asking about him." Christy grins wide. Daryl likes her teasing.

"Rex is going to whip yer ass in San Angelo. He always does." Maria is smug in her remark.

Daryl glances at Maria one more time, then over at the larger cowboy. And now back on Christy, he's playing along with them all for fun now. "Well, if he wasn't your brother, Christy, I might not like you so much…" He smiles at her again, offering her his best charm. She smiles warmly back. She's attracted to him.

"You're a real idiot…you know that?" Maria isn't buying his charm. She looks at Christy. "C'mon, let's go somewhere else."

Daryl's cell phone buzzes. He glances at the screen, it's from his dad, Cal. He looks back at Christy. "Hope to see you in San Angelo next weekend." He's being honest in his remark.

"You will. I'll look for you." Christy nods her affection and turns away.

Daryl looks at the text message from Cal on his phone. Bright black letters filling the screen: "You can only be a Champion if you think like a true Champion! Go to San Angelo to win!" Daryl looks at the message another couple seconds, reading it again, he shakes his head and looks up toward Christy.

She's already gone. Walking out of the bar with Maria and the others.

Daryl clicks Cal's message off.

Going back to the bar.

5
NEMESIS

CIRCUIT FINALS - SAN ANGELO, TEXAS

IT'S A FULL HOUSE WITH A BOISTEROUS RODEO CROWD sitting inside a large indoor coliseum. Television camera crew of about twelve camera operators, assistant camera personnel, boom and sound men, are covering the event throughout the arena and inside the rodeo announcer's booth.

Images of cowboys warming up and bulls pacing the livestock pens are on their television monitors. The rodeo announcer, a man in his early fifties, with graying sideburns and thick goatee, is standing in the announcer both watching the activities behind the bucking chutes. He sticks the microphone up to his open mouth. "Hello rodeo fans! We're here in San Angelo, Texas with the Southwest's top bull riders!"

Daryl and Rory stand near the bucking chutes wiping rosin on their bull ropes. Daryl sees Christy sitting in the stands above them with Maria, he teasingly waves at them. Christy smiles warmly at him.. Maria shakes her head in disgust.

Rodeo announcer leans toward the open window in the announcer booth. "Only ten bull riders will earn points for the World Championships in Las Vegas."

Daryl glances back toward Christy, pulling on his bull strap—as now, Rex Winslow, age thirty, Christy's brother, same height and weight as Daryl, a serious bull rider with passion, approaches Daryl and Rory with two teammates. All showing some real swagger and competitiveness. Rex sees Daryl looking up at Christy sitting in the stands.

"She's way out of your league, asshole." His expression is taunt and cold.

"Rex? Hey, good to see you. Thanks for stopping by, guess you missed me, huh?" Daryl can't stand this guy. He's shoving it down his throat. Rex is ready.

"What the hell are you doing in San Angelo? You're too old to be riding bulls anymore." Rex is giving Daryl his cold stare.

Daryl looks right back at him. "Someone has to keep you honest and straight, Rex. Keep you in your place." Their eyes are locked on each other. "Isn't that right?"

Rex isn't buying into it. "Old timers like you, Daryl, don't know the first thing about being honest."

Daryl's face tightens, the two other teammates are staring at Rory, who has his bull rope clenched tight in his hands, waiting for some action to happen at any moment.

"Word of advice, Weathers. Leave my sister alone, she's not for you. She needs a real man in her life. Not some washed-up bull rider." Rex is serious, Daryl watches him and takes a step toward him.

"I am a real man." Daryl is mentally pushing Rex.

"Besides, your sister is pretty hot lookin', and single again. I'd like to spend some time with her…alone."

"Don't be a shithead!" Rex steps right in front of Daryl only inches away. Rory pushes between them.

"All right, enough already!" He glares at Rex and the two teammates. "We're here to ride bulls, not fight each other in front of the crowd."

"Stay away from my sister! Do you hear me!" Rex is worked up and ready to fight Daryl.

"Or what? It's gonna break your heart if I have a date with her?" Daryl throws it back hard. Rex starts for him again, Daryl standing firm and bumping his chest, Rory grabs Daryl, the two teammates grab Rex, pulling the two angry bull riders apart.

"You need another taste of losing!" Rex is trying to jerk free from his teammates.

"Not from you!" Daryl shouts at him. They struggle to break free and try to get at each other again, the two teammates pulling Rex away, Rory still holding a secure grip on Daryl. Rex and his teammates are about fifty feet away now, pulling Rex across the contestant area. They don't want them to fight.

"Okay, Rory, enough already! They're gone!" Daryl is still worked up. Rory loosens his grip.

"Then quit trying to act like you can kick his ass." Rory releases Daryl, who steps several feet away from him. Watching Rex moving away across the contestant area.

Daryl looks at Rory. "That guy's been in my face since he started riding bulls!"

"He's made the World Championships five times! You haven't made it once!" Staring at Daryl. "Go beat him in the damn arena. That'll shut him up." Daryl looks at Rory, angry, frustrated, absolutely determined to beat

Rex today. But he's got to get his head wrapped around the game.

Daryl grabs his bull rope and stalks away toward the bucking chutes. Rory watches him walk away—then turns and kicks the arena fence out of his own frustration. Tired of keeping watch over Daryl.

————

A MUSCLED BULL RIDER IN THE ARENA FINISHES A DECENT ride, scoring a seventy-two, not spectacular, but an honest score. The bull rider jumps off his bull and trots to the arena fence, as the bull is herded by the two pickup men on horseback to the livestock exit gate.

Daryl approaches his riding chute; there's a big red monster of a bull waiting inside the gate. Daryl looks at the big beast, watching his actions, gauging him, assessing his movements. He waits a moment, then climbs onto the fence and steps over, sitting on top of the big red bull. The chute crew is wrapping the bull rope around the massive animal. Daryl slides his cinch hand into the rope with a firm grip.

He has a different look now with a serious game face on. Rex has made his point. Daryl has decided that he is here to beat Rex and ask his sister Christy to date him again. The bull moves underneath him. Daryl touches the jeweled cross around his neck and rechecks his cinch hand. The gate man is watching him. Daryl relaxes, he feels confident. He lets the bull settle, then nods to the gate man.

Loud crash of the chute gate swinging open!

Daryl and the big red bull burst into the arena! The mighty beast tries to unseat Daryl, spinning hard, then bucking and power driving Daryl forward over its shoulders toward the arena floor. Daryl is sitting tight, he's up for the challenge. He wants to win this ride. The bull jumps and stands straight up on its front legs; Daryl is literally vertical to the arena floor on the back of the beast. The red bull drops and kicks and spins, Daryl sticking to every move...four seconds...five seconds... Daryl is out-riding and out-thinking the massive red beast...six seconds...seven seconds...Daryl is almost making it look easy!

Eight-second buzzer rings! Daryl pulls his hand free and dismounts, hitting the arena dirt floor on his two feet. The bull is still spinning and kicking, he notices Daryl in the arena and starts for him, the rodeo clowns are trying to get his attention. The monster is almost on top of Daryl, who instinctively steps aside and dodges the red beast, then sprints over to the arena fence and climbs on top. Sitting there watching the monster of a bull run around the arena. Daryl waves his hat in the air over his head. The red bull is pushed toward the exit gate by the mounted pickup men. The crowd goes wild, clapping and cheering loudly. The rodeo announcer waits for the scoreboard to light up overhead. The number pops up in a flash of light—eighty-six! "Eighty-six points for Daryl Weathers! A great ride!"

Daryl is on cloud nine. He drops over the arena fence into the contestant area. Rory approaches and knuckle-bumps him. Kaboom! He pretends there's a large explosion of awesome energy and power surrounding them. "I told you, damn it! Beat him in the arena!"

Daryl grins and laughs. "You were right!" He smiles some more, watching the cheering crowd, then looks for Christy, who is standing and clapping. Rex watches Daryl looking at his sister in the crowd from across the contestant staging area. He's also got his game face on, he rosins his bull rope, moving toward the bucking chutes. Rex is ready to ride.

He climbs over the chute fence and sits on the back of a large black Brahma bull; the animal has been dehorned. Rex is determined and ready. He nods at the gate man. The gate swings open. The black beast leaps out of the chute. Rex is firm in his seat.

Daryl and Rory watch Rex's ride from the other side of the arena fence. Rex is making it look too easy. The black bull twisting and turning, bucking, kicking, trying to dislodge Rex, who isn't going anywhere. Rex sticks with the bull, who now swings left and bucks again, it quickly turns right and kicks out, trying to gouge Rex with its sawed-off horn stumps. Rex looks like a professional bull rider; it's a strong ride.

Daryl is impressed, but hoping his own score will be higher. The eight-second buzzer sounds, Rex unstraps his hand and jumps off the back of the black monster, landing on his two feet like Daryl did. The crowd is shouting, clapping and cheering. Two great rides back-to-back!

The rodeo announcer shakes his head with amazing approval.

"Wow! Another great ride by Rex Winslow!" The score pops up on the scoreboard overhead and the judges mark another eighty-six points. "Eighty-six points! We have a tie on the leaderboard!"

Daryl stares across the arena at Rex now standing below the announcer's both waving his cowboy hat around over his head at the crowd. They are still clapping and cheering. "Looks like we are going to have a tiebreaker ride off!" The rodeo announcer has the crowd excited and wanting more. Daryl, a little frustrated and disappointed that he didn't win the go-round straight out, turns away and heads for the bucking chutes.

Country music singer and former champion bull rider, Chris Ledoux's upbeat tempo *"Hooked on an Eight Second Ride"* begins to play mid-song over the loudspeakers:

...He's addicted to danger...ruled by passion and pride...to pain and fear he's no stranger...but his lust needs to be satisfied...hooked on an eight second ride...

Daryl approaches the bucking chutes and steps over the fence, sitting on his last bull of the day. He knows this one either makes him or breaks him. The announcer says his name again and the crowd begins to loudly clap and cheer, hollering Daryl's name, chanting, "Ride that bull! Ride that bull!" Daryl can't hear them; he's totally enclosed into his own peripheral zone now.

He pulls his cowboy hat down tight, waiting a beat. The large bull underneath is getting anxious. Daryl has his cinch hand tight in the bull rope. He exhales, the silence in his own mind is bliss. He waits a moment, then nods. Gate flies open!

Daryl and the bull jump together through the open gate. The bull is a feisty beast with powerful legs. The animal starts bucking, then spinning like a toy top; everything goes to Daryl's left, which is his strong side. He rides the little twister around and around...four seconds...five seconds...six seconds. Suddenly the little bull stops in its tracks, almost dislodging Daryl, who amazingly sticks tight to his seat...seven seconds...Daryl has his heels dug into the bull's wide shoulders, his hand tight in the bull cinch.

Eight-second buzzer sounds. The bull begins to buck and kick again, Daryl unloads off from him to one side, landing on his two feet again. The little bull spins and stops, staring at Daryl like he's going to charge him. The rodeo clowns are moving toward the bull to help, Daryl stares right back at the bull. "Bring it, you little prick!" The bull charges forward, then veers away, just missing Daryl and trotting for the exit gate.

The overhead scoreboard lights up. "Ninety points!" The rodeo announcer is just as stunned as the crowd. "What a ride for Daryl Weathers! He takes the lead again!"

The crowd is shouting and screaming; everyone is stunned by another great ride. Daryl is pumping his fist in the air, moving toward the contestant's gate to exit the arena. Rory is standing on the other side of the gate. Daryl looks toward the bucking chutes and sees Rex loading on his last bull of the day.

Daryl throws his hat across the arena. "Yeeesss, sssiir-rr!!" He shouts as loud as he can, all jacked up and excited. He looks up and sees himself on the big video board hanging over the arena floor. The crowd is still screaming their approval. Daryl runs over and scoops up his cowboy hat, waving toward the rodeo fans. Christy smiles from the grandstands. It was a great ride, and she has renewed feelings for Daryl. Rex is sitting on his bull in the bucking chute watching Daryl, who now turns and gives Rex a big "eat that shit" grin as he clears the arena.

In the living room at the Weathers' ranch, Cal stands on his bad leg dressed in ranch work clothes with his arms folded. He watches the replay of Daryl's ninety-point ride on the television screen in the room. Daryl looks like a world champion bull rider. Cal is impressed and happy for his son. He has a big smile on his face. He knows Daryl has one more ride tomorrow, the final day. He grabs his cell phone and texts Daryl. "Nice ride,

Cowboy!" Cal looks at the television screen, the cameras are on Daryl leaving the arena pumping his fist. Cal sends another text. "You can do better!"

Daryl moves back into the contestant's area waiting for Rex to take his last ride of the day. He hears his cell phone buzz and looks at the message from Cal. Daryl misses the first part of the text and sees only the second part: "You can do better!" Daryl's expression tightens, the message knocking the wind from his sails, as now Rex and his last bull blast from the chute gate!

Rex is all over the bull, anticipating every move. The bull twists and turns, bucking hard. Rex rides him like he's done this hundreds of times before, which he has. Daryl is watching from the sidelines, looking through the arena fence rails, his face shows a renewed competitiveness, he wants to beat Rex. He wants Rex to fail. The eight-second buzzer sounds, Rex easily dismounts landing on his two feet again, the bull kicks some more, then trots away. It's a good ride, the crowd is clapping, shouting and yelling.

The rodeo announcer stands in the booth waiting for the scoreboard to light up and the judge's score pops up on the scoreboard. Another eighty-six ride for Rex.

"Here we go, folks. Eighty-six points again for Rex Winslow. He matched his last ride!" The crowd is cheering loudly; they just witnessed four great rides in a row. Daryl is watching Rex hold his arms wide apart over his head, working the crowd. Daryl has bested him on the last ride of the day and is in the lead now, but Rex knows there's still one more day and one more ride.

The rodeo announcer summarizes the day's events. "Daryl Weathers will hold on to first place for now. But, don't forget rodeo fans, tomorrow our top ten cowboys go for one more bull ride to earn the top prize money and get a chance to make the National Finals in Las Vegas!" Rex drops his arms back to his sides again and exits the arena floor through the contestant's gate. He's moving directly toward Daryl, abruptly getting back into his face.

"You got lucky on that last ride!" He glares at Daryl, staring him down.

"Is that what's bothering you?" Daryl is now right back in Rex's face, getting just as close, the animosity between them building higher again. "Oh, no! Daryl Weathers might beat Rex Winslow at the San Angelo rodeo, one of the best bull riding events in Texas, waa, waa..." he taunts Rex, who steps forward right into Daryl's face. His anger building.

"Don't get your hopes up, old man! You're going down tomorrow!" Rex tries to look as angry as possible, which he does well.

"It's my turn to win, not yours, Rex!" Daryl is glaring back just as hard at Rex. Who quickly brings it back, playing mental games with Daryl.

"Weathers, we both know you'll cave under the pressure on your last ride. You always do."

"Not this time!" Daryl is holding his ground. Just inches from Rex, who is looking for another way to get under Daryl's skin.

"You're just like your daddy! He was a choke artist and so are you!" Rex pushes it over the top.

"You sonsabitch!" Daryl lunges right for Rex, grabbing him by the collar. Rory and two of the bucking chute crew are pulling them apart. "Leave my father out of this!" Daryl is shaking Rex at the collar, who has a wide grin on his face. Rory and the two bucking chute crew finally separate them from each other. Daryl releases Rex's collar. He's completely angry.

Rory is pissed off at them both. "Stop it already, we're here to compete against each other, not fight!"

Rex is looking right at Daryl now with an even bigger grin. He knows he's mentally hurt Daryl, who is crazily and wildly besides himself, almost forgetting he's leading Rex and the others. Rory holds Daryl back for the second time today. The bucking chute crew start pulling Rex away, he's not struggling this time, the mental damage has been done. He knows how to hurt Daryl.

"Leave it in the arena! How many times do I gotta say that to you?!" Rory pushes Daryl the other way.

"I need a drink!" Daryl is furious. He turns and looks back at Rex.

"No, you don't! He's just working you over. Can't you see that?!" Rory knows exactly what Rex is trying to do. He knows Rex wants to win at any cost.

"Yes, I do!" Daryl grabs his bull bag; he spins around staring at Rory. "And don't tell me what I can and can't do!" He looks at Rory another moment, visibly shaken, and then turns away.

Heading for the exit doors.

6

BUSTED RIDE

DARYL AND RORY SIT NEXT TO EACH OTHER AT A BUSY bar in San Angelo. Daryl is on his fourth drink; he guzzles the remainder of his whiskey. Rory doesn't like him drinking like this, not today, he's leading the bull rider's line up. He's got to compete for first place tomorrow.

"Drinking like this isn't going to help you."

"It'll calm me down." Daryl motions to the bartender for another refill.

"That's number five. Drinking this much is going to make you slower. It always does when you drink heavy. You're in first place. That jerkoff Rex is just trying to get into your head is all. You gotta know that?" The bartender brings another drink; Daryl grabs the glass of whiskey.

"It's only one ride." He sips on the fresh drink.

"Why do you let him get to you that way? He knows exactly how to raise your temperature another ten degrees." Rory is trying to make this work. Daryl has a chance to make the world finals.

"It's not him." Daryl looks into his whiskey glass, staring at the amber liquid.

"Excuse me?" Rory stares right at Daryl, who takes another swig of his drink.

"He's right." Daryl shifts in his seat, looking at a couple of pretty cowgirls on the other side of the bar.

"What are you talking about?" Rory isn't sure where Daryl is going with this. He's not sure why he is trying to explain to Daryl, a bull rider who's been riding for eighteen years, how to behave in the final round to win.

"I can't win. I know it." Daryl looks at the pretty cowgirls.

"Why are you saying that?! That's bullshit!" Rory stares at Daryl.

"I'm afraid." Daryl looks over at him. A genuine look of anxiety covering his face.

"Of what?!" Rory is really confused now, not certain what Daryl's talking about. He watches his former mentor, trying to see through his falling shield of armor.

"Of beating my daddy." Daryl keeps looking at Rory for a moment.

Rory stares back at him, almost transfixed. How can Daryl be afraid of beating his own father?

"Your daddy wants you to win! Why would you feel that way!" Rory almost shouts it out; Daryl is being so lurid and unsensible.

"And why does he want me to win? So, he can take credit for telling me how to ride bulls. He wants to hold that over on me. Just like everything else he holds over me." Daryl is saying how he feels. Even if he's a bit mixed up and way too sensitive.

"Are you crazy or what?" Rory is completely upset with Daryl. "You're here to beat Rex Winslow, not your daddy. Who cares if he takes some credit for helping you learn how to ride bulls?" Rory just isn't understanding Daryl's logic right now. It's obvious that it has something to do with all the whiskey.

"You'll never understand." Daryl finishes his drink and drops the mixed-drink glass hard on the bar top. He glances over at the pretty cowgirls again and sets some money on the bar. "I'll see you tomorrow for the show-down. Don't wait up for me." He starts toward the cowgirls as Rory watches him in complete disappoint-ment. He doesn't want Daryl to throw the bull-riding lead away. Not now.

———

DARYL MAKES HIS WAY INTO THE CONTESTANT AREA. RORY stands there in his bull riding chinks with both of their bull riding bags sitting on the ground nearby. He's ready to ride, but what about Daryl? The bull rider ranks have thinned out now; there's only six bull riders left for the final ride. Daryl approaches Rory, he sees Rex standing across the way putting on his riding chinks.

Christy sits above them all in the stands. She sees Daryl and smiles at him; he smiles and waves back. Rory isn't smiling. He's upset that Daryl isn't taking this seri-ously now. He never made it back to the motel room last night and he's flirting with Christy, Rex's sister. It's insanity.

Rex sees the attention his sister is giving Daryl. He looks over at his competitor with a defiant fixed expres-sion on his face that he is going to beat him today, then almost grins. Daryl grabs his bull bag and unzips it. He pulls his bull rope out. It's been cut in half! He looks around, confused, glancing at Rory who also is surprised, then looks back across the contestant area at Rex, who gives him an "eat that shit" grin.

Rex nods at Daryl and drops an open pocketknife with a sharp four-inch blade sticking out one side into his own bull bag. Daryl suddenly looks sick and ill. One of the chute bosses, a dark bearded heavy-set man in his forties, walks toward Daryl. "Weathers, you're riding first, get ready to mount up."

"Someone cut my bull rope in half." Daryl holds up the damaged equipment.

The chute boss sees the cut rope. "I've got one hanging by the chute gate. C'mon on, let's get ready." He starts toward the bucking chutes. Daryl nods his understanding; he glances at Rory who is standing several feet away getting ready for his own ride.

Rory looks at the cut bull rope wrapped around Daryl's hand. He gives him a "don't worry about it" look.

"It's just a bull rope. Focus on the ride."

Daryl shrugs and turns away following the chute boss to the bucking chutes.

Inside the second chute stands a medium-sized bull. Daryl is surprised, he got the luck of the draw, the bull looks like an easy ride. He just needs to look good for eight seconds and score. The chute boss hands Daryl the backup bull rope. It's thinner and shorter than the one he's used to riding with. Daryl nods his thanks and steps over the chute fence, dropping down, and sitting on top of the medium-sized bull. The animal almost acts like Daryl isn't there. It doesn't shuffle around or paw at the dirt. Daryl tries to get comfortable with the borrowed bull rope, it's not the same fit with his hand in the cinch.

The chute crew tie the rear flank strap on the bull, and it suddenly starts kicking and trying to buck. The crew tightens the strap. Daryl suddenly loses his focus and feels unsettled. He's trying to find the right seat on the back of the beast. The bull settles down for a moment. Daryl waits patiently and repositions himself on the bull's thick back. He can feel the bull tighten up beneath him. Suddenly, Daryl doesn't feel good about this ride. He's overthinking the game.

Rory sees Rex watching Daryl from the other side of the contestant area. Rory is flashing an ugly grin and the pocketknife again at Daryl sitting on his bull. Rory starts toward Rex. The gate man looks at Daryl, waiting for his nod. The jeweled cross around Daryl's neck is bothering him for some reason. He grabs it and tries to stuff it inside his partially opened shirt. The bull is starting to get anxious again, scraping his hooves in the chute. Daryl pulls his hat down tight; it's time to go. He nods.

The gate swings open and Daryl comes out marking the bull and sticking tight on his back! The bull is all piss and vinegar, not the mild animal Daryl first met in the bucking chute. The bull bucks and begins to spin right— Daryl's weak side. The bull lurches and bucks and keeps spinning right, the thinner bull rope is sliding through Daryl's hand, he's beginning to lose his seat—

Cal is standing in front of the big-screen television in the family room at the ranch. He starts coaching Daryl like he's done many times before while watching him ride: "Get your head in the game! Watch your balance! Don't let him shake you loose! Keep yer seat!" Cal can see that Daryl is starting to slip from his seat.

The bull is spinning like a wild toy top out of control. Small and muscled, quick and tempered, the animal is trying everything to throw Daryl off his back...five seconds...six seconds...Rory is watching through the arena fence as he moves toward Rex. "Hang on, damn it!" He sees Daryl's hand slipping out of the bull strap, he's leaning forward and then sideways with each spin, but it's not enough…seven seconds…

Cal is watching Daryl on the television starting to come undone. "No! No! Take that power away from him! Don't let him buck you off! You're almost there!"

Daryl loses his seat and falls too far forward. The angry little bull throws its head back and smashes Daryl in the face! Busting his cheekbone. Daryl is knocked off the bull. The eight-second buzzer screeches over the arena. Daryl crashes into the arena dirt hard. He didn't make the time. Cal is upset, then realizes that Daryl might be hurt. His leg suddenly gives him grief; he grabs it in pain.

Christy, sitting in the stands, jumps to her feet. The feisty bull leaps high in the air and kicks Daryl in the ribs, it spins again and starts butting Daryl across the arena floor with its horns and head. Daryl is in vivid pain, he screams out, the rodeo crowd is screaming in fear and surprise, the bull is attacking Daryl relentlessly. Several spectators in the crowd are standing with their hands over their mouths, stunned. What looked like was going to be an easy ride for Daryl, the bull rider points leader, is now a disaster.

Christy watches it all in disbelief, the three rodeo clowns are trying to fight the bull, to get him to attack them and leave Daryl alone. They finally get the bull's attention, and the two pickup men on horseback chase the bull away toward the livestock exit.

Rory moving along the fence, sees Daryl lying on the arena floor, hurt and injured. He walks right up to Rex who is also watching, not expecting the bull to injure Daryl in that fashion. "Hey, I didn't expect that…"

"Asshole!" Rory punches Rex as hard as he can in the mouth! Rex collapses and hits the floor.

Cal is standing in front of the big television screen still watching the cameras pointed at Daryl, who is lying on the arena floor, not moving. "Get up, son! Be strong!" Disappointment and now fatherly concern are written all over his face. The paramedic techs run into the arena, approaching Daryl, who now rolls over and has lifted himself into a sitting position in the dirt. His face is bloody and mangled; he holds his ribs. The medics come up to him, both are aged thirties, average size, one a man and one a woman with her dark hair tied in a knot behind her head. She kneels beside Daryl. "Try not to move. Let us check you out. Where does it hurt the worst?"

The medics both start to reach for Daryl, he waves them away. "Don't!" Daryl grits his teeth and exhales, he manages to stand on his own two feet. The rodeo crowd is more surprised, clapping and cheering that he's not hurt worse. A big zero sits in the scoreboard over the announcer's booth.

Two of the rodeo clowns approach Daryl and the medics. "You okay?" One of the television cameras is focused on Daryl's bloody face now, screening the image overhead above the arena floor.

"Help me out of the arena." The rodeo clowns and the medics help Daryl move through the thick dirt; he walks slowly toward the contestant's exit gate. Daryl is not going to be carried out of the arena. The crowd is clapping and softly cheering their approval. Happy to see that Daryl can move on his own. Cal watches the television big-screen at the ranch; Daryl's bloody face is close up on the screen.

He grunts and painfully steps over to a row of shelves on the side wall filled with bull riding belt buckles, trophies, and photographs. There's a framed photograph of the family, Cal, Audrey, Tommy, and Daryl as boys, taken by the other bull rider on the day Cal was hurt in Oklahoma City. Cal stares at the photograph, rubbing his finger over Audrey's faded image. A sad reminder of what he once had and lost.

Daryl is helped through the gate by the two medics; the rodeo clowns stand back inside the arena. Daryl is broken and deflated. Rory moves toward Dary, helping the medics, "He's my traveling partner." He holds Daryl up under his arm, finding a place to sit. Daryl is starting to get weary. He sees two other bull riders helping Rex get to his feet. Rex is rubbing his jaw.

"What happened to him?" Motioning toward Rex.

The medics are starting to check the severity of his injuries. The male emergency tech asks a couple questions. "Can you breathe okay? Looks like your ribs are bruised, possibly fractured." The female medic touches them, and Daryl winces. She nods at the other medic. Rory leans down closer to Daryl's face.

"Rex tripped and fell. I helped him with a left hook to the jaw. He deserved it."

Daryl grins and tries to smile, but it hurts too much; his cheekbone is crushed, and his face is already swelling. A rodeo doctor, fifties, a handsome, clean-shaven man, arrives on the scene and starts checking Daryl over. "Okay, let's give him some room." Rory steps away. One of the medics is wiping Daryl's bloody face off with a wet rag, the medics are waiting for the doctor's assessment. The doctor starts checking Daryl's cheekbone now that he can see it better, then touches his ribs, Daryl flinches in sheer pain again. The doctor now checks his head for any kick marks from the bull. There's several around his scalp. "We need to get you to the hospital. I can't do anything more for you here."

"I'll be fine. I've had worse." Daryl is trying to tough it out.

"You might have a concussion and at least three of your ribs are probably broken." He pulls Daryl's eyelids open and checks his lenses with a small flashlight, the irises are starting to widen in shock. He touches Daryl's face. "Your cheekbone on this side is shattered. You're going to need a couple of surgeries to repair it." He stands and looks at the two medics. "Get him loaded in the ambulance and over to the emergency room. I'll call it in." The medics nod and the man leaves them to get the stretcher on wheels.

Christy has come down the stairs toward the bottom of the steps, she leans over the railing above Daryl and the others, watching Daryl. He can't smile, as he painfully raises one arm and offers a slight wave toward her. Christy gasps a little holding her hands at her mouth.

Rory looks closer at Daryl, his shattered face, broken ribs, swollen eye, and busted spirit. Daryl is a real mess. "It's time to retire, Daryl. You got lucky that little bastard didn't kill you today."

Daryl tries to look at Rory, he can barely hold his stare. "It's Rex's fault. I couldn't keep my hand in that small bull strap they gave me. I almost had him." He looks painfully over at Rory.

"No, you didn't. He beat you from the moment you left the chute." Rory is blunt and honest. "You were beat before you even got on him. I could see it in your face."

Daryl looks at him the best he can with one eye open and knows Rory is telling the truth. It's hurtful to admit. Both inside his head and around his broken outside injuries. "The difference between your daddy and you, Daryl...he always had heart. He wanted to win and be a champion. To be the best. You've never had that motivation." He watches Daryl a little closer. The honesty of his statement absorbing Daryl. It's time for Daryl to stop riding bulls. He got lucky today that he wasn't hurt worse than he is right now.

Rory picks up their bull riding bags. The male medic arrives with the stretcher. Daryl is looking at the ground, he can't lift his head anymore, he's in too much pain. The two medics and Rory lay him on the stretcher; the medics strap his body down tight. They roll him toward the contestant's gate exiting the arena. Rory follows them close behind.

Daryl is done riding bulls for now.

7
BROKEN PRIDE

Back at the ranch, Cal stands in the riding arena near the large horse barn with a sorrel color horse and lunges it around on a long rope. Almost like his hold on Daryl, who comes up behind Cal and stops. He's bandaged and bruised; his face is grossly swollen and purple. Cal doesn't turn around. He keeps working on the sorrel color horse around the arena. Daryl watches the horse training for a moment.

"You were right." He's trying to stay clear of Cal and the horse.

"Was I now?" Cal continues to lunge the sorrel horse around the arena. He still doesn't look over at Daryl, his bad leg gives him grief, but he mans up and bears the pain. Daryl watches a bit more respectful now.

"I've never tried to be a champion. To be the best. I've always just wanted to get by. To make the next rodeo." Daryl is finally confessing his rodeo ways.

Cal works the sorrel another moment, then slows the horse down and lets it come to a walk. The horse breathes a little heavier and exhales catching some air.

"And, how's that feel? Cal finally looks over at Daryl, the expression on his face is set firm and determined.

"Not worth a damn." Daryl stands there beat up and damaged. He watches his father for a few moments. It hurts Cal to see him that way.

"Look at you…what a mess." Cal is shooting straight. Daryl doesn't respond. His one eye barely open, his face purple and bruised with red marks. Cal holds the sorrel horse at the length of the lunging rope. He looks at Daryl again and now tries to show some compassion through his disappointment. He tries to be softer now and more appreciative that his son is not hurt worse than he looks. "It was never easy for me. Raising two boys and being married to a beautiful woman. I was always worried another cowboy would take her away." He watches Daryl, who is just holding his composure. "I had to practice riding bulls every day. To get myself into the right state of mind and not worry about the other things in life when I was in the bucking chute." Daryl is staring at him; he's never heard these words from his daddy before. "I had to always convince myself that I was better than the others."

Cal moves toward the sorrel horse, pulling on the lunging rope and bringing the animal closer toward him. He unclips the rope from the halter around the sorrel's head and grabs a lead rope tied around the horse's neck. He clips it to the horse's halter. Daryl is still quiet. Cal rubs the sorrel's face, keeping the animal calm. "I had to convince myself that I was better than the others. That I was worthy of being a champion." He rubs the sorrel horse, turning toward Daryl. "Then it was all taken away from me after I rode that monster of a bull that almost killed me."

Daryl stares at his father. He now sees Cal's anguish

and real hurt inside. Something he's never shared with his sons. "You were meant to be a bull rider, Daryl, from the first moment I stuck you on your first steer." He steps toward Daryl, looking at his damaged son's face, his cheek, his eye, and his ribs. "You always had that God-given gift...a natural talent is the best term."

Daryl exhales softly and nods his head.

"I know..." His guilt is finally coming forward now. He shifts uneasily in the dirt, kicking one of his boot heels through the soft sod. "I never took it seriously. I'm sorry."

"I'm glad you're done riding." Cal still has the sorrel horse on the lead rope.

Daryl digs his boot toe into the dirt and touches his cracked ribs, the pain is intense, they hurt like hell. He looks back over at Cal, he wants to change his ways with his father. He glances away and looks around the open ranch, the wide pastures, rolling countryside and beautiful skyline. The only home he has ever known. The same place where his father tried to rebuild his own ruined life.

"I just never wanted to be like you." Daryl looks back at Cal. He's trying to be sincere. "I know, I messed up."

"Was I really that bad of a father?" Cal watches him. He wants the truth.

"No...I see that now." Daryl's face shows guilt and shame. He wants forgiveness.

Cal touches his bad leg; it's obviously bothering him from lunging the sorrel horse. He moves closer to Daryl pulling the sorrel gelding behind him, his breathing a little spaced apart.

"There are two kinds of people in life, son. Doers and quitters. I didn't raise a quitter." He stares at Daryl, who looks straight back at his father's honesty. Cal starts to move past his son toward the barn. Daryl steps in front of him. He reaches out and takes the sorrel's lead rope.

"I'll put him away." Daryl wants to make amends and be helpful. At least today.

Cal watches Daryl another moment, then releases the lead rope. Daryl offers a light smile and nods. He turns around and leads the sorrel horse away. His ribs are giving him excruciating pain, but he's back home to help his father. Cal watches him walk toward the barn.

He's glad Daryl is home.

———

LATE AFTERNOON SEVERAL DAYS LATER AND DARYL IS slowly, and painfully, stacking two-string hay bales into a large hay pile near the side of the horse barn from the back of an old pickup truck with its rusted tailgate down. The sun is starting to drop across the open spaces of the ranch and casting a gorgeous orange glow across the open fields and pastures. The fifty-pound hay bales are the only thing that Daryl can manage to pick up right now. He uses his good arm and unhurt side, trying to protect the cracked ribs on the other side of his chest.

Daryl is soaking wet in sweat and covered in hay pieces. His face is still bruised and marked, but it's healing. He reaches inside his open, soaked cowboy shirt with only three buttons attached on the lower part of the shirt and frees his necklace with the silver chain and jeweled cross. He pulls the last hay bale from the old pickup truck and swings it onto the hay pile. The pain is almost unbearable. He tries to wipe off some of the hay pieces from his clothing and work jeans. He grimaces and clenches his teeth, then reaches into his pants pocket and pulls out a couple prescription pain pills, popping them into his mouth. There's a plastic bottle of water in the bed of the truck. He opens the cap and guzzles the pills down.

He slams the tailgate closed then steps toward the driver's side of the cab of the pickup truck, opening the door and pulling out his silver whiskey flask. He guzzles to help cover the pain. The whiskey is soothing.

————

INSIDE A DARK COWBOY BAR, THERE'S AN OLD MIRRORED wooden bar back from the turn of the 19th century, filled with thick shelves full of hard liquor bottles of all types. Neon beer signs hang from short chains on the walls around the local tavern, where the bar top stretches almost twenty-five feet across the floor of the room. The bar top is made of a thick three-inch slab of pine wood coated with a shiny lacquer finish. There are several barstools standing against the bar and about ten square tables with wood chairs placed around the open dance floor area. Daryl sits on a stool at the pine slab bar top and toys with his whiskey.

There's about a dozen other customers inside the bar, all drinking and having conversations. Daryl swirls the whiskey around the short glass he holds and looks up at one of the three television screens placed up behind the bar. It's on a local news channel and there's a recap of the circuit finals in San Angelo—and now a replay of Daryl's big wreck. He's completely surprised and embarrassed.

Several of the tavern patrons recognize Daryl on the television screen. The news station plays the wreck multiple times from different angles. The words on the bottom of the screen telling how Daryl was the leader of the bull riding points score and lost it all on the last ride when he got thrown and injured. The screen now shows his nemesis Rex Winslow as the winner of the competition, beating Daryl. Daryl sees the recognized stares from around the bar and digs his head further down toward his glass and guzzles his whiskey. The bartender pours him another drink.

————

DARYL WRESTLES A SMALL STEER TO THE GROUND NEAR AN open fire. He coughs hard and touches his sore ribs. They are still very painful. His face is still marked with red lines, but the swelling is gone.

Hector Martinez, mid-thirties, a Mexican cowboy with a small wide sombrero covering his black hair, works for the ranch. He steps toward Daryl and the small steer with a sizzling hot orange glowing branding iron and singes the young cow's hide. The steer bawls for its momma in complete surprise and pain, trying to jerk free from Daryl. Hector pulls the hot iron away and Daryl releases the steer. It runs away and is returned to the herd by another Mexican cowboy. Daryl tries to stand, he coughs again, grabbing his ribs.

Tommy and Cal riding together on horseback, move several more steers toward the branding fire, all the youngsters separated from their mothers. Tommy rides a tall dark gelding horse, and Cal is on his favorite dun horse. Daryl grabs the next bawling calf, he winces in pain, trying to not show the hurt. Cal rides up closer and sees Daryl struggling with the young calf.

"Keep him calm." Cal throws the words down over Daryl.

"I'm doing my job. This is about the fifteenth one we've branded." The calf struggles harder, Daryl is trying to suck up the pain in his ribs, his face shows hurt.

"Let Tommy help. You need to heal."

"I don't need help!" Daryl shouts the words out, struggling with the steer, his response more in pain than anger.

"From up here, it looks like you do!" Cal makes it very clear, then quickly steps down from the dun horse, it's almost painful to watch as he staggers over, and pushes Daryl aside, grabbing the steer and pinning him to the ground. Hector singes the steer with the branding iron. Cal releases the calf.

"Bring me another."

"I can do this!" Daryl is upset that Cal doesn't think he can help.

"Bring me another calf!" Cal doesn't have time for an argument. The branding work needs to get done. Tommy rides up on the dark gelding pushing a couple steers forward. He sees what's happening, as Cal grabs the second steer and pins it to the ground, the pain in his leg is intense, but Cal ignores it. Daryl looks up at Tommy who shrugs and shakes his head, as Hector brands the next calf with the hot iron. Cal releases the steer and grabs the next one.

Daryl turns away and pulls his whiskey flask from the back pocket of his jeans. He grabs a couple pain pills from his front pocket and pops them in his mouth. He takes a long swig while washing them down. The liquid calming his shattered nerves. The pills are more than he needs. Cal and Tommy both see the drinking. Neither one likes to see Daryl drinking whiskey and popping pills while working. More calves are bawling nearby. Hector singes the next steer.

Cal leans away and lets it loose.

———

Daryl mucks horse stalls in the large barn. He's got a wide pitchfork rake and a wheelbarrow half full of horse crap. He's sweaty again, wet and tired. He looks to still be hurting a bit. He drops some horse manure from the pitchfork into the wheelbarrow and grabs his side. He drops the pitchfork in the wheelbarrow and pulls more pain medicine from the front pocket of his pants. He swallows several of the pills all at once, then takes a swig from the silver whiskey flask from the rear pocket of his jeans. He shakes his head getting the pills down his throat. He places the flask and pills back inside his pants pockets. His eyes are dilated and his face looks red and flushed.

Cal steps into the barn from the bright outdoor light through the wide sliding doors in front. He pulls the sorrel gelding by its lead rope and places the horse back into its stall and slides the gate shut. He drops some grain into a small feeding tray, the gelding excited to get the treat, starts munching on the food.

Cal looks over at Daryl. He knows he's been drinking and taking pills again. "How ya doin'?" he asks firmly, already knowing the answer.

"Whatta mean?" Daryl grabs the pitchfork and scoops up another full load of horse crap, He drops the load in the wheelbarrow.

"How does it feel working again for a living?" Cal sets the lead rope on a hook by the sorrel gelding's stall gate. He takes a breath to control the pain in his bad leg.

"Seriously?" Daryl steps from the empty horse stall and faces his father. Cal can see his eyes are a bit red and swollen wide from the booze and pills. He's soaking wet again. "It sucks." Cal watches Daryl turn around and scoop up another rake full of horse shit and drop it in the wheelbarrow.

"There's nothing wrong with hard work." Cal steps toward the empty horse stall.

"I know that." Daryl doesn't want to have this conversation right now. He slides more crap onto the pitchfork.

Cal waits a moment. "I see you're still popping those pain pills and drinking. Why do you have to do that when you're working?" Cal watches him.

"I need something right now... Not sure my ribs are healing right just yet." He coughs and Cal can see the hurtful grimace on his face. He knows how that feels.

"Don't keep mixing those two vices together, son. You won't be able to tame that beast." Cal is watching Daryl and offering real advice.

"Do you think anyone really cares? Besides you?" Daryl is staring at him.

"Does it matter?" Cal is being honest again. Daryl looks at him a bit harder. He wants to tell Cal to just leave him alone. He'll figure it out by himself, good or bad. He digs into another pile of horse droppings and tosses it into the wheelbarrow, trying to satisfy his father. Cal doesn't want Daryl to hurt himself anymore. He waits a moment, then turns away. Leaving Daryl to clean up the horse crap.

———

CAL STANDS INSIDE THE RANCH HOUSE IN THE FAMILY room near the rodeo trophies and belt buckle case. An Oklahoma City Championship rodeo trophy sits on the shelf next to the family photograph. The trophy is dated from 1997, the year before Cal was permanently injured.

He reaches for the image of pretty Audrey with their two young boys, Tommy and Daryl. He holds the photograph of his family, looking through the glass frame, trying to remember his world before he was hurt and before Audrey got sick a couple years later and passed away. There was nothing he could do for her, except drink away the pain of watching the deadly cancer eating her alive. Every day she tried to be brave, and he tried to hide. He couldn't live with his beautiful wife rapidly dying, he loved her so much.

Suddenly, he does something his boys haven't seen him do in their adult lifetimes. Tears swell in his eyes, and he expresses real emotions, apologizing right to Audrey's face. "I'm sorry, baby, I screwed up so badly." He takes a deep breath. "The drinking and staying away from home all the time, I just lost my senses. I couldn't handle the pressure of my bum leg and your deadly cancer." He touches her face, the image smiling at him. "I'm so sorry that I couldn't make you feel better." He kisses her image and holds it there a moment. Now his head and chest hurt. He taps his chest, then pounds on it once and takes another breath. His eyes are moist, showing genuine regret of the lost time that he threw away with Audrey and the boys after his career ending injury when he started drinking. When he should have spent the last couple years of Audrey's shortened life making her feel loved by him again.

He sighs deeply and sets the picture back on the shelf. An anger almost sweeps over him, as he looks at the Oklahoma City Championship Trophy, a reminder of his personal commitments. Yet, he couldn't do the same for the woman he loved, not being with her all the time in her last days.

He waits for a moment, looking at the trophy and the reminder of his selfishness, then angrily throws the trophy across the room smashing it into several smaller pieces.

He takes another deep breath.

8

DARKNESS FALLS

THE END OF THE DAY. DARYL, WITH A DIRTY FACE AND grimy hands, is fully sweaty and wet from the ranch work and chores all day. He sits at the outdoor patio table on the back porch. The sun is dropping lower just above the high patio walls that surround the back porch but is still hanging over the western horizon reaching across the ranch. Daryl drinks from a regular size glass, his third whiskey of the early evening. A partially empty whiskey bottle sits on the table near him.

Cal approaches Daryl from the back door of the ranch house. He's carrying the photograph of Audrey and the boys. He sits across the patio table from Daryl and slides the photo and frame over toward him. "You remember this picture? Oklahoma City 1998?" Cal looks at him.

Daryl pauses a moment, then takes the picture frame and looks at the images closer. "Sure, how could I forget? The day of your big wreck, the day you started giving up on our mother."

"She was so beautiful…" Cal is staring across the porch.

Daryl stares at the photograph, looking at the image of Audrey, himself, and Tommy as young boys. "I really miss her, you know that, right?" He waits a moment, looking back at Cal, the dropping sun lighting up his face. "Why did you let her go like that at the end of her life? Not spending time with her when she needed you most. I'll never understand that?" He watches his father. Cal looks over at Daryl.

He can see Daryl's slightly drunk, the whiskey bottle almost half empty. He fixes his eyes right onto Daryl's face. "I loved the rodeo sport more than anything else in the world, except your mother. And you boys." He waits for another moment. "I loved her so much."

"You sure didn't show it at the end. She was hurting and you weren't there to comfort her. We did everything we could." Daryl remembers the lonely nights his mother was at home by herself with only the boys around.

"You think I don't know that? That I didn't care then?" Cal stares at Daryl. "I was confused and hurt after my accident. Then she got sick. I wanted to be with her…" He keeps looking at Daryl, he's trying to show remorse and compassion. "I didn't know we would lose her so fast. I never understood it all." He takes another deep breath, almost a gasp of air, his breathing is getting a little harder to maintain.

"You left her to die. How could you have done that to her?" Daryl pours himself another drink. His ribs are still hurting; the whiskey is making the pain go away and making him say things he shouldn't. A familiar sequence of events that his father once went through years ago.

"I loved your mother more than anything in the world," Cal stares at Daryl trying to be honest. He has trouble catching his breath again. He touches his chest, Daryl doesn't notice. "I wanted to be a world champion, to be the best in the sport. Your mother wanted that also for me. She was wonderful." He waits, slowing his breathing. "It all was taken away from me after all the hard work I had put into rodeo. Then she was gone."

"You could have brought her home and let her die with all of us by her side. You never saw her at the hospital. The last two weeks of her life. Then we buried her here, Grandpa dug the grave. Where were you?" Daryl remembers his feelings as a boy when Audrey passed away.

"I'm not the one who gave her the cancer!" Cal suddenly grows angry; he tries to calm down. "I couldn't fix her. I wanted her to live, not die like that!" He glares at Daryl, his long-term guilt choking him for trying to drink away his wife's illness. "I tried hard, to make it right...I bought the ranch...I started working the cattle to make a living...so we all could have a good life." His face is redder now, a vivid expression of hurt, shame, and remorse. And a strong feeling that he got cheated in life.

"I want to hear you say it." Daryl swallows most of his drink and grabs the whiskey bottle again, topping off his glass, he stares at Cal. "Say it, damn it!"

"Say what?!" Cal is confused. He's struggling to breathe normally. Daryl doesn't notice.

"The apology you owed her!!" Daryl shouts it across the patio table. He's incensed and a bit inebriated.

Cal stares at Daryl, who takes another drink from the whiskey glass. The alcohol has taken control. Cal can't help but feel he's looking at himself twenty-six years ago. He's suddenly gasping for air. He moves forward in his seat trying to catch more air into his lungs. He shouts the best he can at Daryl. "At least I never quit! Not like you!" He throws it back as hard as he can at Daryl.

"You sonsabitch!" Daryl lets it all loose.

Tommy is standing nearby inside the barn open entrance; he's putting the unsaddled dark horse into its stall. He can hear the loud shouting between Cal and Daryl off the back patio porch. He slides the gate shut to the horse stall and hangs the horse's halter and lead rope on the tack hook in front of the stall. Tommy starts moving toward the wide front doors of the barn, walking outside and toward the back patio. He hears more shouting; the setting sun is covering his concerned face.

"Watch your mouth!" Cal stands, shaking now, barely able to stand on his bad leg, his breath is restricted, his chest is throbbing. He starts to say something else, then realizes he's having a heart attack! He grabs the edge of the table, standing there. Daryl is too caught up in his own anger and remorse to realize what is happening to Cal.

Daryl stands there defiantly. "You never cared for her! Not when she got sick! And you know it!" He's pushing the truth the wrong way. He throws his drink across the outdoor patio against the high wall surrounding the patio, the glass shatters into a dozen pieces, the whiskey flying everywhere.

Cal is trying to tell him he's having a heart attack. Daryl isn't paying attention, he glares one more time at Cal who Daryl thinks, is looking angry at him, not terrified he's dying. He turns and storms off the porch, going into the house. Cal can't breathe; he's gasping for air.

Tommy opens the rear gate of the high walled patio. He sees Daryl going into the ranch house. Cal loses his balance at the patio table. He tries to shout; his chest is exploding inside. His head is growing lighter. He's slipping away to unconsciousness. "Daryl!" he finally yells, falling down onto the patio deck and totally collapsing. Tommy runs over to help him.

He's shocked and surprised.

Not sure what Daryl just did.

———

DARYL DRIVES THE OLD HAY TRUCK WITH THE ROTTING tailgate into the gravel parking lot of the local cowboy tavern bar. The old truck slides to a hard stop in the loose gravel. Daryl is sitting in the driver's seat staring at the tavern door entrance. He picks up his silver whiskey flask sitting on the seat next to him and uncorks the lid, taking another drink and popping another pain pill.

He swallows and opens the driver's door, sliding out of the truck. He drunkenly slams the door shut, just as an ambulance with flashing lights and loud siren wailing, screams past the cowboy tavern. Daryl watches the ambulance and lights drive past. Not the slightest aware that it's going to their ranch to pick up Cal. He stumbles toward the tavern entrance and goes inside the bar.

He makes his way to the thick pine slab bar top and plops down on an empty stool. The bartender recognizes him and brings his favorite whiskey with a glass, pouring a large drink for Daryl. A very pretty cowgirl, early thirties, with auburn hair and a tight-fitting blouse, stands at the bar a few stools down. She's being annoyed by a large rancher, late forties, he stands tall, well over six feet three inches in height and is dressed in his well-worn ranch clothes. He wears a wide cowboy hat stuck over his short hair. The pretty cowgirl turns away from the rancher who's trying to talk to her. She recognizes Daryl as the local bull rider and smiles at him.

Daryl, a bit more drunk, takes a sip from his fresh whiskey at the bar and slips off his barstool. He staggers over to the cowgirl, standing between her and the tall rancher. "Howdy there, darlin'." Offering his best cowboy introduction and smile. "I'm Daryl. What's yer name?" The pretty cowgirl likes the attention. She's relieved the aggressive rancher is standing on the other side of Daryl.

"Hey there, Daryl." The cowgirl looks at him. "I'm Melody." Ignoring the tall rancher, who's still trying to talk to her from around Daryl's back. He becomes quickly irritated.

"Whoa there, cowboy! What the hell, huh? I was talking to this pretty cowgirl before you." He moves around Daryl to face Melody.

"She's with me now." Daryl turns toward the tall rancher, who can see he's been drinking heavily. Daryl's eyes are glossy and partially closed, his face is more flushed red.

"You sure got a smart mouth, mister." The rancher steps toward Daryl, ready for a fight. Daryl wavers on his feet, he can barely stand straight. Suddenly, the tall rancher recognizes Daryl. "Wait a minute! You're Cal Weathers' boy! I watched you get your butt kicked in San Angelo!" He sees the red marks and scars still remaining on Daryl's face from the bull wreck. "I see you're still wearing some of that hurt on your face." He laughs. "That little bull really wiped your ass."

"Maybe so, but I earned it." Daryl is trying to be amusing, but the alcohol is winning.

"Not the way I saw it." The rancher steps closer and grabs Daryl firm by the arm. "Why don't you get yer sorry ass out of here while you can. You're drunk. This girl is with me." Daryl stares straight at the rancher, two bulls locking horns. The pretty cowgirl sees it coming from a mile away.

"Oh, shit…" She steps away.

Daryl swings his free arm and punches the tall rancher in the face! The bigger man surprised, falling backward, then quickly collects himself and lunges toward Daryl, grabbing him in a tight bear hug, spinning him around backward and they both crash onto one of the tables, smashing it apart, they hit the floor among all the debris.

The rancher sits up over Daryl and pops him in the mouth. Daryl tries to swing back and misses. The bartender doesn't want this in the cowboy tavern. He comes out from behind the bar trying to stop the fight. The pretty cowgirl, Melody, is watching in hopes Daryl doesn't get too hurt. Several bar patrons move out of the way for cover. Two tough looking cowboys, both late thirties, both thinned and muscled, rush over to the crashed table and try to help the bartender break up the fight.

Daryl jumps up swinging, and he connects hard, hitting the rancher a second time. Then swings again and hits the bartender. The two tough looking cowboys grab Daryl, pulling him away from the rancher, as he steps forward and hits Daryl again in the face. Then he punches him right in the ribs! Daryl shouts in sheer pain, his ribs hurting again. He screams and kicks the tall rancher in the nuts between his legs.

The rancher shouts and cusses. Daryl headbutts the first cowboy and pops the second cowboy in the nose with a solid hit. He can fight. He turns around, as the bartender with a bloody lip, swings a pool stick and cracks Daryl on the top of the skull, the pole shattering in half into two broken pieces. The stick pieces bounce across the tavern. It's lights out for Daryl as he falls unconscious to the floor.

———

DARYL SITS IN COMPLETE MISERY AND EMBARRASSMENT IN a small jail cell in the local Sheriff's station with a big lump on his lip and a fresh bloody gash swelling across the back of his forehead. The jail cell reeks of alcohol, urine, and puke. Daryl's cowboy hat sits next to him on the hard metal bench. Three other cellmates sit around him, two keeping to themselves, trying to sober up. The third man in the cell is watching Daryl, he acts like he recognizes him.

One of the two men ignoring Daryl has thrown up in the small metal sink on the back wall next to the metal toilet. Daryl glances at the third man again and wants to tell him to look the other away but decides one fight is enough for the night.

A sheriff's deputy, short, about age forty, solid built with a shaved head and his badge pinned on his uniformed shirt, comes into the drunk tank holding area. He stands in front of the jail cell door. He looks in the cell at the inmates. "Daryl Weathers?"

Daryl looks up and waits a moment, then responds. "Huh, yeah. That's me." Daryl is trying to hold his head straight. But it really hurts from the pool stick blow.

"You got a phone call." The sheriff deputy watches him, then sticks his key in the cell door.

Daryl slowly rises as the deputy unlocks the latch on the jail door, keeping an eye on the three others inside. He steps back and waits for Daryl to walk through the cell door, then locks it closed again.

"This way." The sheriff deputy escorts Daryl down the narrow hallway on the other side of the cell past a couple other jail cells with several other drunks sitting and lying inside. They reach a pay phone at the end of the short hallway. The receiver is lying on top of the phone off the hook. "Three minutes, that's all you got." The sheriff deputy steps away and goes through another closed door into the primary sheriff's office. There's a wide window in the wall looking into the short hallway. Other sheriff deputies are taking calls and doing their business around their desks and tables in the office.

Daryl reaches for the receiver on top of the phone. "Hello...?" He doesn't know who is calling.

"Where the hell have you been?!!" It's Tommy on the other line. He sounds very upset.

"Tommy?!" Daryl is a bit surprised, he glances down the hallway at the jail cell, and through the glass window into the Sheriff's offices. "You comin' down to bail me out?"

"He's dead, Daryl! You sonofabitch! What the hell did you do?!" Tommy is standing in the family room and shouting at the other end of the phone.

"Who's dead?!" Daryl looks a bit confused. His head is throbbing now.

"Daddy! You stupid dumb ass!" Tommy isn't holding back.

"Wait?! What?! <u>Our daddy</u>?!" Daryl's face grows taut and shallower. His flushed expression and narrow eyes clenching together tighter.

"I found him on the back patio! He was having a heart attack when you walked away! I saw you leave him there and go into the house!"

"Don't say that!" Daryl is completely at a loss now. "I didn't know he was having a heart attack!"

"Damn you, Daryl! You killed him!!" Tommy is still shouting louder into the phone.

Daryl stares at the wall behind the phone. He's at a complete loss to Tommy's words, he can't believe what he's hearing. He turns around again, tears are swelling in his eyes, he doesn't want to believe what Tommy is telling him. Guilt is swarming all over him, having yelled and shouted like that at their father, making him angry and upset. He now realizes that Cal wasn't being angry at him, he was having trouble trying to speak to him, he was having his heart attack before he walked away.

"I, I don't know what to say, Tommy. I didn't mean to hurt him. You know I wouldn't do that to him." Daryl is in tears now, the words are difficult to say. "I'm so sorry, Tommy…"

"You're an asshole! I hope you rot in that damn jail cell!" Tommy angrily hangs up.

Daryl is staring across the hall through the window of the sheriff's office. He's shocked and stunned. He can barely stand now, his legs giving way. He slowly slides down the wall next to the pay phone. He drops onto the cold cement floor underneath just sitting there. There are no other words. His father is dead. He still grasps the phone receiver; the short cord is stretched taut above his head and his outstretched arm.

Daryl is crying now; the tears and pain are overbearing. He can't believe the loss of his father after he argued with him. He feels his own injuries and disappointments. The alcohol has always been in charge. He knows he should have stopped drinking a long time ago. He saw his father abuse himself with alcohol. His lips begin to quiver. He begins to shake and shudder. He's being overwhelmed with grief.

He closes his eyes, and the tears come harder. He tries

to take a breath, to make sense of it all. He releases the phone handle and puts his hands over his face. Devastated and damaged.

"Daddy...I'm so sorry..." He's crying, he can't stop. The pain and alcohol in his body are overwhelming him now. He tries to cowboy up. To stop hurting and crying. To be a real man.

But he can't.

He cries harder.

9
LAST RESPECTS

A DECORATED WOODEN OAK COFFIN WITH HUCKLE BEARER handles sits on a metal gurney covering the open hole of a fresh dug grave that is laid out next to an older grave site with a faded white stone marker that says: "Audrey D. Weathers, Wife and Mother, born August 12, 1962 – died May 22, 2003."

The gravesites are side by side together in a private family burial plot on the Weather's ranch. Green grass covers the small cemetery under several beautiful oak trees. A brighter stone marker for the new gravesite has been inscribed as Calvin L. Weathers, born April 12, 1960 – died October 6, 2024.

Daryl and Tommy, both dressed in their best cowboy clothes and frock coats, are standing about fifteen feet away from each other at the burial site. Neither wears a cowboy hat. Rory and his family, wife Sarah Jane, age thirty-six, attractive brunette with shoulder-length hair, and their two daughters, Ashley, age eight, and Miranda, age six, both with brown hair and beautiful brown eyes, stand between Daryl and Tommy.

Hector and some of the other full-time ranch hands, along with about a dozen other mourners from the surrounding ranches, all dressed in their cowboy pants, shirts, buttoned vests, and full-length dresses, also stand near the gravesite.

Pastor Lemmon, an older, thinner man, age seventies with a gray, balding hairline, is offering last rites and a final eulogy for Cal. The pastor holds his Bible open opposite of the family and mourners; he says his final words and closes the book. "May God rest your soul and watch over you for all eternity. Amen."

"Amen." The majority of the mourners mouth the last word together and close the ceremony. Pastor Lemmon now motions toward Tommy, who starts past the coffin first, dropping a small handful of dirt inside the open gravesite. Rory and his family follow next, then Daryl, who pauses for a long moment at the open burial plot, trying to collect his thoughts. He stares at the oak coffin and then tosses some dirt into the gravesite and moves past to where Tommy and Rory's family are standing together. The other mourners are now filing past the coffin and open gravesite giving their last respect for Cal, a good man who always tried his best.

Daryl moves toward Tommy, standing in his long shadow under a wide oak tree, he watches the other mourners moving past their father's coffin. He waits for a moment, then turns toward Tommy. "I just wanted to say, that—"

"Shut the hell up, Daryl!" Tommy turns toward him, angry and disappointed, his face clenched tight. "Daddy was right! You're a bum and a loser! Always has been, always will be!" He stares directly at Daryl. "I want you off the ranch!"

"Tommy, please..."

"Leave! Now!" Tommy is giving Daryl no room for choices. He stares at Daryl another moment, then turns and walks away, greeting several of the mourners. Daryl watches him go, then looks over at Rory, who shakes his head with disappointment in Daryl. He puts his arm around his beautiful wife, Sarah Jane, and their young daughters, ushering the family toward the other guests and to Pastor Lemmon to offer their thanks. None of the other mourners look at Daryl as they walk past. No one says a word to him.

Daryl stands there alone. He waits and watches the others offering their blessings and last rites. He looks back at his father's coffin.

Then turns and walks away.

———————

LATE AFTERNOON ON THE SAME DAY OF CAL'S FUNERAL. The sun is dropping slowly over the open pastures and rolling countryside of the ranch. The old pickup truck with the rotting tailgate comes roaring into the front yard area of the ranch house and slides to a hard stop, crashing into the front steps of the house and making a large banging noise! The ranch house porch shudders hard. The driver's side window is rolled down and looking through the dirty windshield, we can see Daryl sitting behind the steering wheel holding the silver whiskey flask. He's been drinking heavily again.

Tommy comes running out of the front door of the ranch house onto the porch. The setting sun almost blinding him, he raises his hand to block the glare. He's trying to see what the heck hit the house. He now sees Daryl sitting in the front driver's seat of the old pickup truck. The front bumper and hood are smashed together against the front steps on the side of the porch.

Daryl opens the cab door and falls out to the ground, he's completely drunk. He holds the whiskey flask in one hand, sitting on his ass. He holds the whiskey up high and guzzles the remainder of the liquid amber, draining the flask. Daryl tries to stand, grabbing the pickup truck door open window to help himself, as Tommy angrily jumps off the porch and approaches him.

"Look at you!" Tommy is furious. "We just buried our father today! What the hell are you doing?!"

"I really loved him." Daryl is hanging onto the pickup door window, he's barely able to stand.

"You never showed it!" Tommy wants to hit him, but not in this state of condition.

"I did everything he asked." Daryl is starting to slur his words. He's beyond help right now.

"You never even tried! Why would you say that?!" Tommy is being straightforward, he knows Daryl is talking through the alcohol haze.

Daryl squints at Tommy through his closed half eyes. He suddenly releases the truck door, lunging forward at Tommy, swinging his fist and hitting him! "I don't deserve this!" They fall together on the ground. Daryl tries to hit Tommy again, drunk and stupid. Tommy rolls on top of him and hits him back harder, then over him, hitting Daryl multiple times in complete frustration.

"You're crazy! And a dumb shit!" Tommy yells at Daryl, then realizing what he's doing, he stops hitting him. Tommy shoves him back to the ground. Daryl lies there, yelling at him.

"I didn't kill him!" The guilt and despair are completely visible now.

Tommy holds Daryl against the ground, his brother's

face red and bloody now. Daryl is a total drunken wreck. Tommy can't stand to look at him anymore. Daryl finally calms, Tommy disgustingly releases him, wiping blood from his own lip, where Daryl hit him. He stands over Daryl.

"I've got cows to feed!" He stares at Daryl, lying there on his back, a total mess. "Get your ass into the house and sleep it off. You're leaving tomorrow." He turns and starts for the barn, leaving Daryl on the ground. Daryl rolls over and spits blood.

He watches Tommy walking away.

———

DARYL STAGGERS INTO THE RANCH HOUSE AND INTO THE family den. The pain, remorse, guilt and anguish coming to the surface again. The sun has dropped over the horizon; there's barely enough light in the room to see where he is going. He stumbles to the trophy shelf and looks at the trophies and belt buckles, all won by Cal. There are a couple trophies that Daryl won when he first started to ride bulls. He looks at the old photograph of the family in the glass frame, staring at Cal in the old picture.

"Why did you push me away?!" He is shaking now, almost unable to stand. "Why did you do that to me?!" He angrily swipes Cal's trophies and belt buckles off the shelves, they all crash to the floor. Daryl almost slips and falls, he grabs the shelf and straightens himself. Then he starts stomping on the trophies, smashing them into pieces under his boots.

"Damn you! Damn you!" He jerks the silver necklace from around his throat, grabbing the jeweled cross and throws it across the darkening room against the other wall. He staggers, trying to keep standing, then trips and almost falls on the trophies broken underneath his feet. He grabs the family photo inside the glass frame. Staring at his mother and father, and now his brother, Tommy. Daryl's eyes are wet and he's crying again, trying to grasp the last images of his happiness.

"I didn't want this! It's not supposed to be like this!" The words spilling forward in a wild drunken slur. He pulls open the top drawer of the bureau cabinet sitting underneath the shelves built above. There's a Colt .45 single-action pistol lying inside the drawer under some white house linens.

Daryl pulls the six-gun out with his right hand, grasping the solid wooden handle. His finger touches the trigger guard. He stares at the family photograph held tightly in one hand and the Colt pistol held firmly in the other hand. He points the gun at the family picture, the barrel stuck right on Cal's face, then he turns away from the shelf and slowly raises the gun, pointing it toward his head.

The overwhelming bitterness and despair of what he has done are completely wrapping their ugly arms around Daryl's soul. There are more tears of anguish and hopelessness, of utter despondency and depression. Daryl feels like he's at the end of the world.

He sticks his finger around the gun's trigger. He stares across the room. The Colt pistol is pointed at his head. Tears fill his eyes. His face is bloodied from the beating Tommy gave him.

Boom! A loud report and flash of gunfire.

The room goes dark.

———

Sunshine and clear skies, as Rory's long truck pulls toward the front of the ranch house. He sees the old pickup work truck smashed into the front porch steps. Rory pulls his truck to a stop and exits the driver's side of the cab, viewing the wreck. He shakes his head in disbelief, then steps up onto the front porch and opens the door, taking a long look inside. He hesitates another moment, then quietly enters.

Rory looks around the front room as he walks through the house toward the family den. He enters the room and sees Daryl lying on the other side of the floor, he's not moving. The smashed trophies, belt buckles, broken dreams, and old family photograph sitting in the glass frame lay around him. There's a lot of blood on the floor and he sees the Colt .45 single-action pistol lying next to Daryl, his hand still wrapped around the grip.

"Daryl?" Rory leans down and removes the Colt pistol from his hand, checking to make sure the six-shooter's hammer is down. He tucks the gun behind his back and gently nudges Daryl. He can see lots of blood near his head, he pushes Daryl over on his back, his eyes are still shut, and it doesn't sound like he's breathing. Then suddenly, Daryl gasps and opens his eyes, gulping down some air.

"You okay?" Rory shakes him some more. He can see the bruises and red cuts on Daryl's face from the beating Tommy gave him. And his own abuse from drinking and falling.

Daryl stirs from his alcohol slumber and coughs. He covers his mouth and coughs again. Rory helps him into a sitting position. He sees the blood matted on his forehead where he fell and hit the trophy case. Cal's shattered legacy surrounds him on the den floor.

Daryl leans back against the bureau with the drawers under the trophy shelves and hacks out the remainder of the night before. He turns and spits it onto the floor among the broken trophies.

There's a bullet hole punched into the wall just above them. Daryl is barely conscious; yet through bleary eyes he sees the broken necklace and jeweled cross lying on the floor near them. He leans forward and scoops it up, stuffing the good luck charm into his front pants pocket.

"Look at you." Rory sits on the floor next to him.

"Leave me alone." Daryl has no idea where he's at or what day it is.

"You need help, Daryl."

"I don't want your help." Daryl wants to stand, but he's too weak. He tries to look at Rory, he certainly recognizes his good friend, but he can barely keep his eyes focused. His vision is blurry and irritating.

"This was your solution. Try to kill yourself?"

"You don't understand." Daryl is now embarrassed and his head hurts like hell. He rubs his eyes trying to clear them, then touches the gash on his forehead.

"Tommy called me this morning. He came in from feeding the cows last night and found you lying here. He left you alone to sleep it off and told me I should come over this morning. So, here I am."

Daryl looks at him the best he can, his eyes are partially closed, he squints through the alcoholic hangover staring at Rory.

"Your daddy was a good man, Daryl. You need to remember him that way." Rory is looking right at him. "He believed in you."

"He made my life a living hell." He looks at Rory the best he can. "I need a drink."

Rory looks at his friend right in the face. He grabs him by the shoulder, squeezing hard, so Daryl knows he's serious. "You're done drinking, Daryl. You need to get your life back together. Yesterday you almost ended it. That's twice in the last two months."

Daryl looks over at him, he doesn't want to listen. He tries to meekly rise. It's too painful. Daryl is completely broken, and it really shows. He flops back down on the floor. "Why are you here anyway?" He looks angrily back at Rory.

"Why do you think? Someone has to help you get yourself together again."

"I hate you." Daryl stares at him, the best he can.

"No, you don't." Rory waits another moment, watching Daryl. He looks pathetic, he's a much better man than this. "I found you a job. It's close, nearby. They breed bucking bulls. Something familiar to you." Daryl stares at him. "Bucking bulls?"

"You start work tomorrow." He rises and stands over Daryl. "So, get yourself sober and cleaned up today. Tomorrow, you start work. I'll pick you up in the morning." Rory looks down at Daryl, who is still staring back at him the best he can. "Tommy says you can stay in your room here at the ranch until you can afford your own place. He's trying to help you, even though he can't stand you right now."

Daryl shakes his head and spits more phlegm out. "Of course he said that. He owns the ranch now." Daryl isn't amused, nor is he certain of where his life is going. He looks up again at Rory, who stands there watching him another moment, then gives Daryl a nod.

"I'll see you in the morning. Get your shit together." He turns away, Daryl can see the Colt .45 pistol stuffed in the back of his pants. Rory exits the room, then out the front door. Daryl hears the screen door slam shut. He sits there on his butt and exhales a deep breath.

Sadly, staring across the room.

10
STARTING OVER

RORY'S PICKUP TRUCK PULLS DOWN A SHORT DRIVEWAY
toward two large metal buildings that are built next to
each other. One is a full-length rodeo arena under a
wide tin roof, the other is a large, covered barn for
horses and bulls, with livestock holding pens attached.

The truck pulls up to the open rodeo arena and stops.
Rory sits in the driver's seat, and Daryl is sitting in the
passenger seat. They both exit the truck, slamming their
doors shut, and meet in front of the truck. Daryl looks
like he is still hurting from the whiskey hangover and
cuts from the day before. He glances around.

"Doesn't look like much of a place, huh?"

"This guy was a world champion bullfighter. Five
years in a row."

"Bullfighter? What's he doing way out here?" Daryl is
moving toward the open arena. Rory is walking right
next to him.

"Raising badass bulls. What else?"

Daryl looks at him, as now, Shawn Cornell, a Black

man, early fifties, slim and fit, clean face, approaches them both from the barn. "You, Rory?"

"Yes, sir. Are you Shawn?" He extends his open hand, and they shake their formal greetings. "This is Daryl Weathers. The bull rider I told you about."

Shawn looks Daryl over. Looking at the cuts and bruises on his face and forehead. "I've heard your name before. You get those from a bull ride?" Referring to the various facial injuries.

"Daryl's a natural bull rider. He can feel the bull's strength and weaknesses better than anyone else I know."

"He tell ya' to say that?" Shawn grins at Rory, looking at Daryl, who hasn't said a word yet.

"What? No...just my opinion."

Daryl still hasn't said a word. He's looking around, checking the place out, Shawn sees him eyeing the livestock pens. "There's plenty of work here. You're welcome to start today." He looks at Daryl a little closer, carefully gauging his stance and manner of appearance. "I could use a good hand."

Rory has a smile on his face. "That's perfect. Daryl's ready to start." He turns to Daryl. "I'll be back later this afternoon to pick you up. That cool?"

"You his older brother?" Shawn stares at Daryl. "You don't talk much, huh?"

"Nope." Daryl finally speaks to him.

"So, you do speak, English. That's great." Shawn is grinning.

"All my life." Daryl looks straight at Shawn.

Rory grabs Daryl's right hand.

"I'll see you after six o'clock." He nods at Daryl, then at Shawn, and turns away going to his pickup truck. The bullfighter and bull rider watching him leave. Shawn looks back at Daryl.

"Okay, let's get you started. We got a lot of work to do." He turns and starts for the livestock pens. Daryl waits a moment, then follows him toward the fenced corrals. Several big monster bulls are grazing on hay and alfalfa in their muddy stalls.

"We mostly provide stock for the local rodeos, but a few of the meaner bulls go to the larger events around the state." Daryl looks at the bulls, there's nothing here that he hasn't seen before. Shawn grabs a wide-mouthed snow shovel and hands it to Daryl. "Your job is to keep these bad boys cleaned up." Daryl looks at him. Not what he was told.

"When do I ride the bulls to get them ready for the newbies?"

"You're not riding right now. Not yet anyway."

Daryl stares at him, then firmly takes the snow shovel. Not what he wants to do, but it's a job. He looks back at Shawn, not sure if this is going to work out.

"When's our lunch break?"

"At lunchtime." Shawn grins. "Hope you brought something to eat?"

"Of course not." Daryl isn't smiling.

"Then we'll start lunch break tomorrow. Bring your lunch then." Shawn grins again, he turns and walks away. Daryl stares after him for a moment, watching him walk toward the covered rodeo arena. He turns toward the bulls standing in their pens. The shovel is ready for action.

———

THE MIDDAY SUN HANGS OVERHEAD IN THE BLUE OPEN SKY, building up more heat and sweat, as Daryl shovels out the bullpens. He pushes a barrel full of junk through the mud and dumps it near a large pile on the other side of the horse barn. Just like back at the ranch. He moves toward another bullpen and comes through the open gate with the wheelbarrow, the bull inside seems unconcerned. Until Daryl pulls the snow shovel off the wheelbarrow and starts scooping crap behind the beast, which suddenly moves toward Daryl. He quickly steps away, his natural instincts again. The bull is now on the other side of the muddy pen. "Easy, big fella, we're just trying to make it nice in here for ya." The bull looks over its shoulder at Daryl, then ignores him and goes back to eating.

Daryl starts shoveling bull poop again, dumping the crap into the wheelbarrow. Shawn watches him work through the open doors of the metal barn. He's cleaning some bull-riding tack. He likes the way Daryl just stepped aside of the big bull with a simple ease. He thinks Daryl might be a good fit in the rodeo arena. But he wants to wait and make sure Daryl is a hard worker.

Daryl hears some activity in the rodeo arena. He scoops up the last pile of the bull crap from the pen and moves the wheelbarrow outside the gate, closing it tight. He drops the heavy load onto the large discard pile and rolls the wheelbarrow over toward the rodeo arena to see what the noise was.

Shawn is there now with the bull riding tack and greeting two young cowboys in their early twenties. Both are new to the sport of bull riding. Shawn's ranch hand, Tony Murratto, about the same age, another black man, loads one of the practice bulls into the bucking chute on the other side of the arena. The first young cowboy, a little smaller than the second cowboy, jumps on to the chute fence and loads over on top of the practice bull. The bull isn't that large, but big enough to hurt someone if they aren't careful in the arena.

Shawn walks through the arena and stands in front of the bucking chute offering some advice to the novice rider. Daryl can't hear them, but he can see the young cowboy nodding his head, as he listens to Shawn. The former world champion bullfighter and owner of the ranch steps away and Tony throws open the gate.

The bull, a smaller breed, starts to buck and kick, he's a moderately aggressive animal, obviously used for beginners to the sport. Shawn shouts encouragement and instructions to the first cowboy, who hangs on and rides the bull for about five or six seconds, then is tossed off into the dirt.

Daryl watches the young rider, then starts rolling the wheelbarrow toward the other side of the livestock pens. Shawn sees him over there.

———

DARYL LIES ON HIS BED IN HIS ROOM AT THE RANCH HOUSE.

There's a bottle of spring water sitting on the nightstand next to the bed. He's reading a bull-riding magazine with plenty of action pictures. He skims through the pages, absorbing the images of the bull riders and nasty bulls at the big money events.

He turns the page and finds a photograph of Rex sitting on top of a large mean bull winning the bull-riding competition at one of the top rodeos and advancing toward the World Championships.

Daryl stares at the image for a few moments. He closes the magazine shut and tosses it onto the floor. He leans back with his arms tucked up over his head. He's still trying to figure out where his life is going from here. He hasn't had a drink in almost a week.

He wants one, but he's committed to sobering up.

At least for a while.

———

DARYL CLEANS NEAR THE BUCKING CHUTES IN THE RODEO arena, then pushes the wheelbarrow to the large crap pile near the horse barn and dumps it out. He's filthy dirty, sweating heavily, his pants are covered in dung and his tee shirt and arms covered in muck. He sets the wheelbarrow aside and grabs a heavy water hose, pulling it over to the arena and connecting it to a faucet to spray some of the dirt down near the livestock pens and under the bleachers.

Shawn is in the rodeo arena with Tony talking to another beginner bull rider sitting on another practice bull. He steps aside of the bucking chute, and Tony throws open the chute gate and the young cowboy and bull are released into the arena. The rider barely makes three seconds and is bucked off. Tony moves the bull toward the livestock exit gate, as Shawn goes over to the young cowboy, grabbing his hand and pulling him to his feet, making sure he's fine.

Daryl starts spraying the dirt down under the bleachers near where the livestock exit gate is set up, there's only about ten rows of seats to sit on. Suddenly, the bull turns and starts toward Tony, smacking into his side and knocking him down. Daryl sees this and turns off the water hose. He drops it on the ground and slides into the arena between the fence rails, throwing his hands up, getting the bull's attention. Tony is holding his side, the bull wants to attack him again, but Daryl runs in between them, waving his arms and getting the bull's attention.

Shawn is standing on the other side of the arena walking with the young cowboy toward the exit gate near the bucking chutes. He hears the commotion on the other end of the arena and turns toward the bull and Daryl, running toward them. The feisty bull charges Daryl, who steps aside, the bull misses him then quickly turns back. Daryl steps aside again, waving his arms in the air, the bull not making contact for a second time. Shawn sees it all.

The bull comes toward Daryl a third time now, as Shawn grabs Tony and helps him to the arena fence. Daryl dodges the bull and runs to the fence, jumping on top out of danger. Shawn charges the beast and moves him toward the livestock exit gate. He slams it shut, then turns toward Daryl who has dropped back down into the arena. Shawn moves toward Daryl.

"What the hell was that?"

"Whatta mean?" He stares at Shawn. "It looked like Tony needed some help."

"You never get in the arena on foot if you don't have a game plan."

"Game plan? I'm sorry, I helped him." Daryl doesn't like where this is going. He starts to turn away.

"You ever fight bulls before?" Shawn is staring at him. Daryl turns back around.

"I've sure rode enough of them to know how they behave."

"That doesn't matter standing here. Not to these ornery bastards." Shawn is watching him. Daryl isn't sure this is worth his time. He starts walking away again.

"That's it? I slap you hard in the face one time and you walk away?"

Daryl stops and turns around. He looks at Shawn. "I'm not looking for trouble."

"You should be." Shawn moves toward him. Daryl digs his boots into the thick arena dirt a little deeper, not sure where Shawn is going with this. He stares at him, making it clear, he's just trying to get by right now.

"What do you want?"

"Do you want to try and fight them? The bulls?" Shawn stops a couple feet short of Daryl. He's got a serious look on his face. Daryl stares at him.

"Why would I do that? I'm a bull rider." Daryl doesn't know what Shawn's looking for.

"From what I just saw, you got the power to fight them." Shawn steps closer.

Daryl stares in his face a little closer. He's still not sure where this is going. "You want me to fight bulls? I thought I was hired to help train the newbies to ride. Which you haven't let me do yet."

"Maybe you can give these ornery animals a little payback for the pain and hurt they've caused you?"

"Are you serious?"

"Come on. I'll introduce you to Violet."

"Violet?"

"He's got a bad temper."

"He really does." Tony joins them from the sidelines, he's okay, just a little bruised on the side. "One of the worst attitudes in the entire lot. I can testify to that."

Shawn grins and extends his hand to Daryl, who looks at him for a moment, then reaches over and shakes his grip. As the three of them walk back across the arena.

———

Shawn and Daryl stand in the middle of the dirt-filled arena dressed in colorful rodeo garb. Football cleats, colorful leggings, funky shorts with yellow handkerchiefs hanging out of their pockets and baseball chest protectors. Neither has paint on their face.

Tony stands above the bucking chute gate and pulls on a pair of heavy gloves over his fingers, pulling them up tight. He grabs the large gate handle underneath him. There's a large, older dull colored bull named Violet standing behind the livestock gate. Shawn shows Daryl where to stand when the gate is opened.

"The first thing ya gotta know is where to position your feet." Shawn shows Daryl how to stand when fighting bulls.

"That looks easy enough." Daryl copies his stance.

"The second thing is body language."

"What's that?" Daryl is watching him.

"You can't be too stiff, and you can't be too loose. Understand?"

"That makes sense." Daryl isn't sure though what that really means. He gets into his bull stance and sticks his hands out in front of him like he's going to "catch" the bull. Shawn isn't amused.

"Don't do that."

"Do what?"

"Stick your hands out like that. You're not catching him."

Daryl drops his hands more naturally to his sides. The large bull inside the livestock gate is getting more excited, he's stomping and pawing on the ground, he wants out into the arena.

"Violet is an old Brahman bull, probably been around more rodeos than both of us combined."

"Why's he got a girl's name?" Daryl is digging his cleats into the dirt.

"I don't know, I never asked him." Shawn motions to Tony to open the gate. "You ready?"

"I guess so."

Tony slides the latch open and pulls the gate up, Violet comes charging out into the arena, all two thousand pounds of muscle and thick fur.

Shawn digs his cleat into the soft dirt arena. "He's gonna charge us but really doesn't want to hurt us." He's stepping toward Violet. Daryl follows him.

"Are you sure?"

"Of course not!" Shawn is grinning and laughing. "He's a ton of angry, old-time bull! He wants to rip your head off!" Shawn prepares to fight Violet.

Daryl is wondering what the hell he's doing in the middle of the arena right now. Violet has a straight line focused on the two bullfighters. He's done this so many times before, he could do it blindfolded. The large beast drops his head and starts pawing at the ground.

"That doesn't look good." Daryl is trying to figure out where to stand, he's watching Shawn.

"Get ready…he's coming hard."

Violet charges right at them. Shawn immediately runs toward Violet and starts working around the bull, getting his attention, keeping his head down. Daryl is terrified. He freezes in place. Shawn sees it.

"Don't stop! Keep moving!" Shawn is running around Violet, shouting at Daryl, who is only about ten feet away. "Don't think, just do it! Get a rhythm! Right, left, right…"

Violet turns and comes charging at Daryl, who starts to move, he stumbles right, then left, Violet whirls past. Then he spins around, still quick for his old age. He comes charging at Daryl again, now catching him and getting underneath him, throwing Daryl high into the air. Daryl shouts in complete surprise, he wasn't expecting that! Ironically, he almost feels at home here. He hits the soft arena floor and drops in the dirt. Quickly getting back to his feet.

"Is that supposed to happen?!" he shouts toward Shawn, kidding around, he's getting an adrenaline rush, getting into the game.

"Keep dancing!" Shawn is grabbing Violet's attention now, touching his head near his big horns.

"What if he doesn't want to dance?!" Daryl is right next to Shawn now, moving back and forth, dodging the thrusts of Violet's massive head.

"He always wants to dance! He's the prince of the ballroom floor!" Shawn runs forward and leaps over Violet's head! Stepping on his massive back and jumping off to the other side! Daryl is amazed and excited.

Tony is watching for the arena fence. "Go get him, Cowboys!"

Daryl starts moving left, then right. Violet catches underneath him again, tossing Daryl in the air a second time, but this time he comes down landing on his two feet, moving again. "Hell yes!" Daryl is thrilled.

"Keep moving! He's gonna keep charging!" Shawn touches Violet on the head again, just like old friends. "Hello, big boy! You're doing great today!" Violet turns toward him. Daryl suddenly runs between them, planting himself right in front of Violet and catching his breath.

"Is it always like this!" Daryl takes another deep breath; he's totally into the bullfighting.

"Every time! Every rodeo!" Shawn dances in front of Violet.

"When do we take a break?!" Daryl dodges Violet again.

"When he gets tired…" Shawn is grinning and playing with Violet.

"When is that?" Daryl catches his breath once more, as Violet charges him again, he quickly steps aside, Violet violently spins and charges him one more time. Daryl just barely jumps out of the way. Shawn is laughing now. Daryl is definitely a natural bullfighter.

"In about fifteen minutes! Keep moving!"

Daryl is sucking on air. He's laughing with Shawn.

He has no idea why he's enjoying himself so much.

———

DARYL SITS WITH SHAWN OUTSIDE OF THE HORSE BARN entrance area. They are both still dressed in their bull-fighter wardrobe. Daryl looks exhausted. Shawn looks at him with a serious thought.

"I put myself in harm's way for twenty-five years saving cowboys."

"You may have saved me once or twice." Daryl winces, it hurts to move. It's a good pain for once.

"We used to be called rodeo clowns because of our wardrobe and makeup." He looks at Daryl and offers a bottle of water, Daryl takes it in appreciation. "Being a bullfighter isn't about being a hero. It's about making the sport respectable, about someone being in charge inside the arena, and protecting the bull riders." He waits for another moment, reflecting on his past. "Regardless of how you feel about some of them. We are the ones that protect them."

Daryl listens, he likes what he is hearing. Shawn is being completely honest and open about the work.

"It's always been about saving lives. If one of us fails, we all fail, and someone gets hurt...or worse...maybe permanently injured...or killed." He watches Daryl, who takes a drink of water from the plastic bottle. He swallows and nods, his eyes set back on Shawn.

"I think I've found something I might want to do for a while." Daryl is looking at Shawn. "Maybe it's my way of making up for all the years of not believing in myself."

Shawn watches him a little closer. He really likes Daryl's attitude. He thinks Daryl could be good at this sport. If he takes it seriously and to heart. "Well, let's try it out a few more times if you want. Either you'll be good at it, or you'll get yer butt kicked hard." He grins and smiles.

"I'm not too old to fight bulls, am I?"

Shawn looks at him and laughs. "Only if you feel too old."

Daryl smiles back. He wants to give bullfighting a try. He's not sure why yet.

11

SECOND CHANCE

GATESVILLE, TEXAS

Nice outdoor rodeo arena with lots of double crew cab pickup trucks attached to horse trailers. Several of the trailers have wide sleeping quarters, most are stock trailers for three to four horses. Several horses are standing, already saddled and tied off to the horse trailers.

Cowboys and cowgirls are preparing for the rodeo, walking around, visiting their competitors, there's country music playing over the loudspeakers around the rodeo arena and grandstands.

There's a four-horse trailer with no horses tied to it attached to a pickup truck on one side of the parking lot. The tack door on the front side of the trailer is wide open and there's someone standing inside. Daryl steps out through the open door stepping into the parking lot. He's dressed as a bullfighter. His face is painted with red and white streaks applied across his cheeks and around his eyes. He's wearing new football cleats, cut-off blue jeans, a loose shirt, stripped leggings, and two colorful yellow wild rags are stuck inside his belt. He's far from a perfect looking bullfighter, but it's a good start.

Daryl shuts the horse trailer tack door and starts toward the contestant's area. Walking past the bronc riders, team ropers, bull riders, barrel racers, and calf ropers. No one appears to hardly notice him and there's not much swagger to his steps. The paint on his face is masking his real identity. It's a new game for Daryl. But he's up for the challenge.

He reaches the bucking chutes at the bottom of the bleachers, the grandstands are modestly filled, not packed yet, but busy enough. The audience is just taking their seats, there's no cheering, no shouting, just locals out for a good time to support their friends and neighbors. It's a summer rodeo event held in town.

Daryl walks through the contestant's area gate and enters the rodeo arena at ground level. This is unfamiliar to him, starting a rodeo on the ground. The arena feels much bigger than what he remembers, even though he's been in dozens of rodeo arenas. The dirt is at least six inches thick and has been freshly tilled and raked, it's a bit uneven and extremely soft. It's not easy to walk through, let alone to run through.

Shawn enters the arena and approaches Daryl near the announcer's booth. He's not dressed as a bullfighter, just dressed in his normal cowboy duds with a champion bullfighter belt buckle wrapped around his waist and a nice cowboy hat. He's not bullfighting today. The local rodeo announcer, mid-thirties, tall and thin, stands above the arena floor in the announcer booth overhead. He grabs his microphone and looks around the growing hometown crowd preparing them for the rodeo event.

"Helllooo rodeo fans! Welcome to the twenty-first annual Gatesville Charity Municipal Rodeo..."

Shawn steps toward Daryl. "You can step out of the arena any time. But, once those gates are open, you're committed. Understand?"

Daryl is watching the crowd fill the grandstands, he looks over at Shawn. "I think it's about time I did something right."

Shawn smiles. "All right then, it's going to be a long day. So, good luck. I'll be watching." He nods and starts to turn away, then pivots back around. "Oh, and one last piece of advice. Don't let the bulls get behind you. That's when it gets rough and you get hurt."

"Ain't going to happen." Daryl has his game face on now.

Shawn grins and nods again, he turns and exits the contestant's gate from the arena. Daryl starts walking over to the bucking chutes. A pickup man on horseback blows past him! Thundering hooves, Daryl barely steps aside from getting run over. That was too close. Suddenly, it all feels real now. Daryl realizes he's going to be in the middle of the action. This isn't the same place as Shawn's small rodeo arena at his practice ranch.

Two bull fighters, Red Small, age thirty-two, short and stocky, the barrel man, and Ajax Wills, age twenty-nine, dressed similar to Daryl, he's a bit taller and skinnier, approach Daryl. Barrel man, Red, runs up and slaps Daryl across the shoulder. "Hey, sorry, we're late! Name's Red Small. I'm the barrel man today!" He extends his hand and Daryl shakes it firmly. Ajax steps closer.

"You're the new guy, huh?" He reaches for Daryl's hand, who grabs it back, as Ajax squeezes hard, then releases his grip and turns away. He starts moving toward the bucking chutes. Red follows, approaching his colorful bull barrel sitting on the ground to the side of the bucking chutes marked with a popular beer logo plastered around the barrel. Daryl follows them, trying to catch up.

"Hey, I didn't introduce myself. I'm Daryl Weathers."

"I know who you are." Red turns around and stops. He looks right at Daryl. "I saved yer ass in Fredericksburg, back in 2018."

Daryl stares at him for a moment, then laughs. "That was a good rodeo. I placed second."

"I remember that." Red grins and knuckle-bumps him. "Not sure why you're fighting bulls now, but you'll be fine. Make sure to use the barrel to protect yerself." He watches Daryl for another moment. "It's just the three of us tonight. It's going to get very real. So be ready." He glances toward the bucking chutes. Ajax is talking with one of the bronc riders. "They're going to run the bronc riders and calf ropers first, then we're up. Are you ready for this?"

Daryl suddenly feels about two feet tall in the wide-open arena as he watches the rodeo crew start loading the bareback broncos into the chutes.

Red looks back at him again. "Let's get out of the way. When the real action starts, just holler if you need to change your shorts." He grins and gives Daryl a thumbs up, sliding through the railings of the arena fence and into the contestant area. Daryl is at the fence now as well. His stomach is suddenly full of knots; he's never felt this way before the start of a rodeo. At least not since he started riding bulls eighteen years ago. He slips through the fence and stands in the contestant area. He feels out of place. He's not in his bull-riding garb and he's not holding a bull rope.

He looks upward into the bleachers. The crowd is

filling up the remaining empty seats now, the rodeo is about to start. The rodeo announcer in the booth above the bucking chutes is telling the crowd to get ready for a great time. Daryl sees Shawn sitting about halfway up the bleachers with Tony next to him. They both wave at Daryl and give him a thumbs-up. Shawn gives Daryl a strong smile and shakes his head. "You got this." Daryl watches him for a moment.

Damn right, I do.

———

DARYL IS GETTING HIS STANCE IN THE MIDDLE OF THE rodeo arena in front of the bucking chutes. Ajax is positioned off to his right side and Red is standing inside the rodeo barrel between them. Three large bulls are loaded in the bucking chutes, and their riders are all standing behind the chute fences ready to load up.

Daryl touches the silver chain and jeweled cross around his neck; he's wearing it again. The crowd has come to life, they have been enthusiastically watching the bronc riding and team ropers, and now the bull riders are up. The wildest event in rodeo is ready to start. Daryl takes a deep breath and digs his cleats into the soft dirt. The first bull rider, early twenties, youthful appearance, climbs the fence and sits on top of his bull, the big animal is not comfortable. The big beast paws the dirt underneath and kicks at the fence behind him. The young rider settles down, then nods at the gate man.

The chute gate bursts open! Bull and rider blast into the arena, Daryl has never been at ground level like this facing two thousand pounds of anger and fury with a rider sitting on its back. The monster bull begins to twist and turn, unleashing its fury like hell and high water, the rider is losing his grip. Daryl tries to stay away from them…four seconds…five seconds…the rider is becoming unhinged. Daryl yells at him, "Keep yer balance!" Six seconds…

Daryl steps toward the bull, ready to step in and help the bull rider. Ajax is doing the same on the other side, as Daryl shouts at the bull rider again, "Stay with him!" Seven seconds…eight seconds…the buzzer sounds loudly, the crowd screaming and cheering in excitement. It was a decent ride.

Daryl is moving closer to the bull, he sees Ajax stepping near on the other side, the bull rider clears his hand from the bull rope and jumps off the beast toward Daryl's side. The bull turns toward him, wanting to gore the rider. Daryl steps between them getting right in the bull's face, coaxing him, teasing him, grabbing the bull's complete attention. Red is watching from the rodeo barrel. Ajax is watching from the other side of the bull. Red is impressed that Daryl is showing no fear. Suddenly, Daryl pivots around the bull and slaps him on the ass! "Over here!" shouting at the bull.

The beast is surprised for a moment, it spins around in a circle, the crowd roaring with more excitement. They don't see that too often. The two pickup men on horseback push their way between Daryl and the bull, moving the animal toward the livestock gates and clearing the bull from the arena. Ajax runs over to Daryl and high-fives him. "That was awesome! You're already fighting like a pro!" Red trots over with the barrel wrapped around him.

"Great job!" He also high-fives Daryl. "You got only ten more ornery ones to fight."

Daryl is grinning at them both, he now feels something running down his arm. He pulls his arm up over his head and takes a look on the back side. The bull caught him with his rear hoof, there's a slight gash, blood is seeping down his arm and shirt sleeve. Daryl stares at the fresh gash for a moment, then laughs out loud. "Hell, yes! Let's do this!"

Running back to get into position.

ABELINE, TEXAS

Another rodeo arena in another town with full grandstands. Daryl is walking outside the rodeo arena in the crowded area where the beer and food vendors are selling their goods. There are several activities for the kids placed around the vendors, like bean toss and ring toss, with fun prizes. Daryl wears his bullfighting gear, his face is painted with red and white lines, and some new paintwork is added. There's a fresh confidence in his steps, as he moves through the crowds. Several school children around ages six to ten run up to him, asking him to autograph his bullfighter picture in their rodeo programs. Daryl happily obliges the youngsters. It's a feeling of maturity and change that he likes. He never thought bullfighting would come naturally to him. This is his fifth rodeo now.

Daryl completes the half a dozen rodeo program signings and looks past the kids. Cody Holden, age eight, typical size kid, is standing near the arena fence across the way. He smiles at Daryl and offers an approving thumbs-up. Daryl likes his new admirer; he's a handsome young boy and almost reminds Daryl of himself when he was that age. He smiles and waves back at Cody, as a female barrel racer, trots her horse past. Daryl steps aside, letting her sweep by, he looks back over at Cody. He's not there.

Daryl glances around and sees Cody walking the other way from him. He grins and nods his satisfaction, moving toward the rodeo arena. The bull riding event is about to start. Daryl needs to get his head on straight and his game face on.

———

LOUD SNORTING AND DIRT FLYING IN THE AIR. DARYL IS IN the middle of the bull-riding action. A massive bull is charging straight toward him. Daryl dodges and then scrambles behind the rodeo barrel. The bullfighter inside watches through the open top. Daryl's painted face and unshaved chin are visible above through the opening. Daryl spins around the barrel twice, the bull trying to hook him with his horns. Daryl jumps on top of the barrel and sits on it. The bull is still chasing him around the barrel, then finally realizes that Daryl is gone. The crowd in the bleachers roar their approval!

Daryl jumps off the barrel, and bullfighter inside stands up and sticks the top part of his body outside the barrel. Pretending to feign his displeasure with Daryl sitting on his barrel. It's a great little play-acting and the crowd loves it, laughing and cheering louder. The pickup men move the bull away to the livestock exit gate. Daryl turns and waves goodbye to the bull, the crowd roaring with more laughter.

He high-fives the barrel man and then notices Cody standing on the other side of the arena fence. He waves at Daryl, who grins and waves back. Cody steps onto the fence rails and climbs to the top of the fence, looking over the top rail into the arena. Daryl suddenly gets a queasy, familiar feeling. The sight of Cody looking at him reminds him of his day in Oklahoma when he watched Cal ride the big black-spotted bull.

Now, Christy, Rex's sister approaches Cody from the bleachers. She grabs him and brings him back down to the ground. Daryl is surprised and is staring at Christy. What's she doing here? Then he realizes that Cody is Christy's young son! She looks through the fence railings at Daryl standing in the middle of the arena but doesn't recognize him with the paint smeared all over his face. She stares at the dashing bull fighter, a bit happy that he waved at Cody. Daryl stares back at Christy, then waves at her. She waits a moment, not sure who the bullfighter in the arena is, but waves back. He seems like a nice enough cowboy.

Just as the chute gate is thrown open and another wild bull bursts into the arena bucking and kicking, trying to throw the rider off its back. Daryl spins around and starts rushing toward the nasty bull, he starts dancing around in front of the beast. Christy watches Daryl fight the bull, she's more than impressed at his bravado, as Daryl moves left, then right, then left again, keeping the bull in check. Christy touches Cody on the back. "Okay, let's go. I gotta get back to work," as they move away from the action.

Daryl is running circles around the bull.

————————

Daryl exits the staging area outside the rodeo arena. The bullfighting for the day is over. The bulls are all put back in the livestock pens. The bull riders are talking to each other, packing up their riding gear, talking about their scores and the bulls they rode. Some are flirting with a few of the cowgirls. Daryl is sweaty and worn tired, one of his shirt sleeves is ripped, but he's better for worse and wear.

He wets some water on one of his yellow bull flags underneath one of the faucets near the restrooms and swipes his face off. Removing some of the rodeo paint from his features. He stuffs the dirty rag in his back pocket and grabs the silver necklace and jeweled cross from around his neck. Stuffing them back into his shirt. He swipes the arena dust and dirt off his bullfighting outfit. Just enough to look halfway decent, as he now moves back into the open crowded area.

Cody suddenly runs up to him. "Hello, again."

Daryl stops and looks at the young boy, he gives Cody a friendly knuckle bump. "Howdy, buckaroo."

"What's your name, anyway?" Cody has his head back looking up at Daryl.

"Daryl. What's yours?"

"Cody."

"Nice name." Daryl watches Cody another moment. He likes this kid.

"My mom gave it to me."

Daryl waits another moment, then responds favorably. "I actually met your mother before."

"You did?" Cody is a bit intrigued and surprised. Daryl grins at him, looking around for Christy. She's not anywhere to be seen.

"Where is your mother, anyway?"

"I'm hungry. How about you?" Cody looks at him.

Daryl watches Cody, not sure how to reply, then digs into his back pants pocket and pulls out one of the dry yellow bull flags. He hands it to Cody. "Want one of these?"

"To keep?" Cody takes the yellow flag.

"Sure, it's yours. I've got a bag full of 'em."

"Do you like hot dogs?" Cody is playing with the flag.

Daryl looks at him. "Sure, who doesn't?"

"My mom makes the best hot dogs." Cody is smiling at him.

"She does, huh?" Daryl is wondering what that means.

"She makes them...*over there*..." Cody points across the walkway toward a bright carnival vendor's booth with the words "Hot Dogs" painted in big bold neon letters above the open glass window.

Christy is standing inside the vendor booth, busily taking orders from the hungry rodeo crowd. Daryl stares at her for a moment, now smiling. He didn't expect this, his mouth is curling on the sides around the remainder of the red paint on his face. Cody grabs his arm.

"C'mon, you can meet her again." He pulls Daryl toward the hot dog vendor booth. They move through the crowded food and game area. Cody now stands outside the hot dog vendor window and waves at his mother. Christy leans through the window looking at Cody. She now sees Daryl standing there to his side.

"Daryl?" She's surprised to see him in his bullfighter gear, now realizing he was the bullfighter in the arena she waved at! "That was you in the arena?" She's genuinely happy to see him. She looks at Cody standing next to Daryl and really likes the look of them standing both together. It feels very comfortable and natural. She smiles at Daryl, looking radiant as ever. Daryl is awestruck.

"Where did you find your friend?" she teases Cody.

"I met him earlier. He's real nice."

"I'm sure he is..." Christy smiles at Daryl and grabs

an order from the cook, she hands two hot dogs to a waiting customer, a mom and her daughter.

Daryl steps closer to the window. "It's great to see you again, Christy." He can't believe his luck. Here's beautiful Christy with no Rex or Maria interfering. Christy looks at him, his dirty bullfighter clothes, the partially smeared makeup removed from his face.

"When did you start bullfighting?"

"About three months ago. I can't get enough." He laughs. He can't stop looking at her. "It's a different world fighting bulls. Then riding them." Daryl isn't sure he said that right.

Christy smiles, looking around the vendor area outside the food booth window. "I had a friend was going to help watch Cody for me today, but she didn't show up." She grabs two more hot dogs loaded with all the toppings from the cook. Handing them to two teenagers.

"I can hang out with him for a while if you want. It won't be a problem." Daryl is offering to spend time with Cody. Christy looks at him.

"I'm hungry, Mommy."

"Uugghh, you're a bottomless pit. You've already had two hot dogs today." She almost laughs. "You want mustard or ketchup?"

"Mustard!" Cody is excited.

Christy looks at Daryl. "You want one too?"

Daryl grins, sure why not. "I like mustard." He smiles at her.

Christy grabs a couple hot dogs and squirts mustard on them both. She leans back through the open window and hands them to Daryl.

"There are some tables over there to eat at. I'll come over in a little while."

"Race you!" Cody grabs one of the hot dogs from Daryl and runs toward the round outdoor tables with umbrellas stuck in the middle for cover. Daryl is all smiles, he looks at Christy, she smiles back very friendly.

"Have fun, Cowboys."

Daryl still can't believe his good luck.

12

NEW LOVE

DARYL FOLLOWS CODY TO AN EMPTY TABLE. THEY SLIDE into the seats. Cody is already munching on his hot dog. There's more mustard on his face than on the hot dog. Daryl grins, watching him.

"What's your favorite part of the rodeo?" Daryl takes a bite out of his hot dog, he's a little surprised, they're actually pretty good.

Cody gives him a look that says, *really?* He speaks with a mouthful of his lunch. "The big bulls. They're scary."

"They are scary." Daryl is eating his lunch as well with a full mouth of food. He watches Cody enjoying his hot dog, not trying to pry too fast, but curious. "So, Cody, where's your daddy?"

"I don't have one." He munches another bite full. His face is a real mess now.

"Really?" Daryl is looking at him.

"Uh, huh, my mommy and him aren't together anymore." He shoves the last of the hot dog into his small mouth, Daryl grins, how did he get all that in there at once?

"Does she have a boyfriend?" Daryl is pushing the best he can.

"Nope. Just me." Cody is munching his mouthful.

"I see…" Daryl takes another bite.

"My mommy loves me." Cody's face looks like a rodeo clown's painted face. Daryl grins and grabs some napkins from the holder on the table and wipes Cody's face, who is smiling, as he wipes the mustard away.

"I'll bet she does." He watches Cody eating his hot dog. He reaches into his front pocket and pulls out his red nose that he wears sometimes when bullfighting. He sticks it on Cody's nose. "Hey, that's a great fit."

Cody is laughing, trying not to spit out his hot dog, he covers his mouth. "I like it."

They laugh together. Daryl swallows the last of his hot dog.

Christy approaches them, she grabs Cody and squeezes his red nose. "Hey, munchkin, that looks great on you!" She gives him a hug and kisses him on the forehead. "You already finished your hot dog?"

"Yep, it was great!" Hugging her back and almost coughing up the remaining mouthful on her. Daryl likes the mother-son love they have for each other. Christy looks at him.

"You could have called me and told me you were fighting bulls now." She watches him. Daryl is careful how he responds.

"Well, it just kind of happened." He smiles at her. She smiles back again.

"Thanks for helping with Cody." She's sincere in her words.

"He's a good kid. We had a great time."

"I like Daryl, Mommy. He's fun."

"Oh, he is, huh?" She tickles Cody, who squeals with delight, laughing.

"I didn't know you had such a terrific boy." Daryl is hoping to get her attention in a good way.

"Well, now you do." Christy watches him, she's completely comfortable with Daryl. She waits a moment, still looking at him. "Cody normally doesn't talk with men. I'm surprised he opened up to you so fast?"

"It's the painted face. Completely irresistible."

Christy laughs, she looks at him another moment, then grabs a paper napkin from the dispenser on the table and leans forward, wiping some of the remaining paint from Daryl's face.

"It certainly is." She smiles at Daryl. She likes sitting next to him. Cody is also smiling.

"I'm working with this rodeo organization for the rest of the summer." Daryl holds his face closer. He likes her touching his face. He watches her some more. Christy pulls the dirty napkin away.

"That's cool. So are we. I started doing hot dog vendor work last summer. It's good money for a single mother." She looks at Daryl a bit closer.

"Does that mean we can hang out together?" Cody excitedly knuckle-bumps Daryl's fist, who gives it back to Cody with enthusiasm. Everyone is enjoying the moment.

"Sure, it does, pal." Daryl likes the whole idea of hanging out with Christy for the summer. He rubs Cody's head. "Guess I'll see y'all tomorrow then?"

"Want to get some ice cream?" Christy is enticing Daryl to spend more time with them.

"Ice cream! Ice cream!" Cody is ready.

Daryl grins and looks at Cody, then sets his gaze onto Christy. "I like ice cream."

Christy grabs another napkin and wipes the rest of the red and white paint from Daryl's face. She looks at him and nods. "That's better. You're a lot more handsome, just like before." She's teasing him.

Daryl smiles. He's already smitten.

END OF THE DAY AND THE RODEO IS OVER. DARYL SITS with Christy and Cody at one of the food tables, the sun has dropped lower, it's almost sunset. Cody is leaning against his mother, sleeping soundly with raspberry-colored stained lips. The sun is throwing the last bright orange rays of daylight over the little boy's handsome face and across the rodeo grounds. There's several vendors and contestants still packing up their trucks and trailers.

Christy explains a little more of her past to Daryl. "When my husband got injured performing, he decided to drink his pain away. He got too abusive, so we had to leave him. That's why Cody is so protective now." She watches Daryl for his reaction. He's thinking of how to best say what he went through as well.

"I was going down that same road after my wreck in San Angelo. Drinking and doing pills, until I started fighting bulls. It changed my attitude." He looks at her, hoping his honesty will make a difference. "I haven't had a drink in over two months. I feel much better for it."

Christy studies him, she's always liked being around him but wasn't certain about his honesty about developing a strong relationship together. She's seeing and hearing a different man in the same skin. "I was afraid when you got hurt in San Angelo. It looked worse than you acted like it was in the arena." She watches him a bit closer. "Do you like it? Fighting bulls?" She stares at him, still gauging his handsome demeanor. "It's got to be a lot more dangerous than riding them?" She waits for a moment.

Daryl looks at her with a big smile on his face. He likes where she is going with the conversation. He takes a deep breath and looks straight into her eyes. "As crazy as it sounds. Yes, I like it better. I feel like I'm in more control of what I'm doing now. Even if there is more risk involved."

Cody moves slightly against Christy, she comforts him, he quickly drifts back to sleep. "What happens if you get hurt? Does anyone care?" She watches Daryl, staring back into his eyes.

He offers a slight grin. "I really don't know. It's all so new to me." He smiles at her and wants to lean closer and kiss her. Christy feels the same way.

"How come you never told me you had a son?" Daryl wants to get more personal now. Christy smiles and looks at him. She's okay with his question.

"Rodeo and kids aren't for everyone. I earned that the hard way." She watches him.

"That's true." Daryl really wants to kiss her. They stare at each other. Christy moves Cody's head, pointing his face sideways out of the setting sun.

"I'm going to have to close up the hot dog booth." She softly laughs. "I never thought I'd be selling wieners at the rodeo." They both laugh together, trying to keep it low, so as not to wake Cody. She looks down at her son. "I haven't seen him this tired in a long time." She swipes his hair away from his face.

"He's a good kid. You're very lucky." Daryl is enjoying their moment together.

"He can be a handful." Christy smiles again.

Daryl leans forward. "He's a boy. What did you expect?" He looks at her and then kisses her on the lips. It's brief, but just enough. Christy looks back and smiles. That felt good.

"I'm sorry if I misled you." She watches Daryl's response.

"Maybe, we could do more than ice cream." Daryl wants to spend more time with her.

"You mean like a real date?" Christy likes the idea.

"Yeah, I've been trying for two years now to take you on a real date." He's grinning wider. Christy likes the feeling together. She laughs.

"I'm pretty busy running the hot dog both right now," she teases him. Daryl leans closer again and kisses her a second time. This time they hold it together for a moment longer.

Christy turns serious now. "Can you promise me one thing?" She stares at Daryl, who is ready to promise her anything in the world.

"What's that?" Daryl watches her. Hoping it's something nice.

"You won't hurt my son." Christy is being protective. She watches Daryl.

"I wouldn't do that." Daryl is trying to be straightforward and honest.

"Please don't say things you can't do." Christy looks at him to see if his facial expression is going to change. It doesn't he's still got the same sincere look.

"That's not who I am anymore." Daryl means every word.

Christy smiles wider now. She's feeling more comfortable with Daryl. She feels she can trust him. She wants him to be a part of her life now. Hopefully for a long time. Meeting him like this in the middle of nowhere must have been intended by God's will.

"Why don't you hang out with Cody tomorrow before you fight the bulls and let me know if you feel any different about us." She smiles again.

Daryl looks right at her. He's feeling like they are going to be together for a while. He puts his hand on her leg and gives her the best bullfighting lingo he can muster under his breath.

"Darn tootin' I can make that happen."

They laugh and smile together.

———

DARYL AND CODY STAND NEXT TO EACH OTHER OUTSIDE the rodeo arena fence in the contestant's staging area leaning backward against the fence rails.

It's a beautiful morning with clear blueish skies and only a hint of the afternoon heat soon to be hanging in the air. Daryl, with his face painted and dressed in his colorful rodeo clothes, gets into his bullfighter stance. Cody is mimicking him. He also has red and white paint smeared on his face. He looks the rodeo part in his cowboy boots and older hat.

"Do I look ready?" Cody is all business and ready to get in the arena. Daryl is smiling at him.

"It takes skill to look ready." He's trying not to laugh.

Cody repositions himself, getting deeper into the bull riding character, his painted face is somber and stern. "Like this?" He stares ahead.

Daryl is grinning, he likes hanging out with Cody. "Yep. Just like that." Cody shows some real swagger. Daryl looks across the contestant's area toward the livestock pens. Several of the rodeo bulls are standing and laying down in their pens. "You ever meet a rodeo bull close up before? Face-to-face?" Daryl looks down at Cody. Who looks back at him.

"Whatta mean?" Cody glances across the open contestant area toward the bullpens.

"Want to meet one?" Daryl is grinning wider.

"Really?" Cody is getting excited.

"Sure. C'mon." Daryl starts walking toward the bulls, Cody enthusiastically follows right next to him. They reach the livestock pens and stand outside the fence near one of the bigger Brahma bulls. A real tough looking fellow with one crooked horn. Cody stares at the mighty bull.

"Can you feel his power?" Daryl is looking at the big beast as well.

"What's his power?" Cody is a bit mesmerized, not sure what Daryl is saying. Daryl looks closer through the fence railings at the big Brahma bull.

"Every part of him, is just wanting to show you who's the boss." Daryl stares at the big bull, he fought him yesterday, he was a tough one to get out of the arena.

"He looks really mean." Cody is staring at the bull munching on hay.

"He is mean." Daryl still remembers barely escaping the crooked horn yesterday.

"Can I touch him?" Cody leans closer to the fence. The Brahman bull stops munching on his hay and looks over at Cody. Daryl likes Cody's style.

"Only if he wants you to." They both look at the Brahma, his eyes are saying touch me and I'll kick you in the head. He snorts loudly, Cody ducks behind Daryl, watching the big beast.

"Is he mad at me?" Cody looks around Daryl at the bull.

"Nope. That's just his way of saying 'hello.'" Daryl has his arm around Cody's shoulders.

"Do you think he likes me?" Cody stares at the big bull.

"I think he knows you're talking about him." Daryl watches the massive beast. He likes the feeling of mutual trust. He glances down at Cody. "Yeah, he probably likes you."

The Brahma bull turns and comes over to the fence, he eyes Cody through the railings. The bull sticks his face close to Daryl and Cody and snorts again, spraying a little snot on them. Cody ducks behind Daryl again, the Brahma turns and goes back to chewing hay. Cody looks back from around Daryl, staring at the big bull. He bravely steps forward and reaches his small hand through the fence slats and touches the Brahma bull on the shoulder.

The large bull barely notices him. Cody smiles, excited. Daryl watches them together, as Cody brings his hand back to his side. He looks up at Daryl, a big smile on his face. "I felt his power."

Daryl smiles back and stares at young Cody for a moment, the familiarity of learning everything brand new when he was Cody's age is returning to his senses. He grins wider. "Don't lose that power."

"I won't. I promise." Cody is looking at the Brahma bull and clenches his fist. He can feel the bull's energy flowing up his sleeve and arm. He looks at Daryl again.

That was awesome.

———

MID-AFTERNOON WITH A BEAUTIFUL BLUE SKY surrounded by partial white and gray clouds hanging overhead. The heat is a little heavier and tougher now. Daryl is wearing his rodeo garb and is dirty from just fighting bulls in the arena. He walks over to the open window of the hot dog vendor booth, the red and white paint is wiped from his face, he wants to look clean for Christy.

She sees him approaching the booth and leans out the window under the big sign reading Hot Dogs while handing a couple hot dogs to some children and looking at Daryl. "Hey, Mister bullfighter. How'd it go out there in the arena?"

"It went great. I only got hit by a couple big horns three times today, nothing serious." He smiles at her. Christy is smiling back. Daryl looks around the vendor booth. "Where's Cody? I saw him watching the bull riding earlier." Daryl is pleased to see Christy again.

"He's with some of the other boys checking out the sheep shearing."

"That sounds like fun."

"Are you hungry?" Christy is inviting him to lunch.

"What's for lunch?" Daryl is teasing her.

"Hot dogs and mustard." Christy smiles, then teases him. "Or ketchup." She grins at him.

"I'll take two dogs with mustard." Daryl likes the closeness.

Christy grins and slides two steaming hot dogs through the window. Daryl reaches for them and touches her hand. Christy doesn't pull it away. She likes his touch.

"What time are we meeting tonight?" She smiles friendly.

"Seven o'clock. Does that work?" Daryl's face is locked in a wide smile.

"That's perfect." Christy is enjoying the moment together again.

"I'll pick you up in my truck." Daryl grins some more, he wipes the mustard on the hot dogs around a little more. He's hungry.

"How about I pick you up in <u>my truck?</u>" Christy looks at him a little closer, she's serious. "I've seen your old beat-up truck with the smashed-in front grill. I don't want to go to dinner in that ugly thing."

Daryl laughs. He likes her honesty. "It's a great ranch truck." He looks at her. Christy's smile is absorbing.

Several other customers come up to the open window, Daryl steps aside and they give Christy their orders. She glances back toward Daryl, who smiles at her and winks. He turns away and takes a big bite out of one of his hot dogs. Raising the food in thanks to Christy.

She grins wider.

———

CHRISTY AND DARYL PULL INTO THE PARKING LOT OF A low-budget hotel driving her Silver Ford F250 pickup truck. It's a newer truck with a wide crew cab and very comfortable seats. Daryl is a bit impressed that it feels so good. It has been a wonderful evening together. They pull up and stop right in front of Daryl's hotel room door sitting five feet away.

"Thanks for the ride. It was a great evening." Daryl looks at Christy and waits a moment, then leans over to kiss her. Christy looks at him coming closer, then passionately kisses him back. Daryl likes the new aggressive attention. Christy pulls away with a big smile on her face.

"Anytime, cowboy." She also enjoyed the evening together.

"Did you like dinner?" Daryl doesn't want to leave just yet.

"It was good Mexican food. How could we go wrong?" They laugh together, looking at each other again. Christy leans over and kisses him once more. "I should get going, I told the babysitter I wouldn't stay out too late." She watches Daryl, she really doesn't want to leave just yet either.

"Cody is a lucky boy. To have a wonderful mom like you." Daryl smiles at her. He wants to kiss her again.

"Thank you." She watches him another moment. "I think you've said that twice now." She smiles a little wider. She likes being with him. "I really did have a great evening."

Daryl smiles back, then unlocks the passenger door and swings it open. He starts to climb out of the cab. Christy suddenly grabs him and pulls him back inside. Kissing him hard.

Daryl tries to keep his composure. He brushes a strand of hair from her face, then kisses her back strongly. Suddenly, they are all over each other, locking their lips passionately and intimately. Lost together in the moment, their bodies close and warm together. Christy starts tugging on Daryl's shirt, catching him by surprise. She's trying to pull his shirt out of his tight jeans to get closer to him. To feel his chest. He helps her pull his shirt out, then starts unbuttoning the middle of her blouse. They are pulling each other's clothes off, Christy doesn't resist. Daryl kisses her more intimately, then he stops.

"Wait a minute. My hotel room is right there in front of us."

"That's too far to walk!" Christy, excited, slides against him closer. Daryl is grabbing her around the waist. Kissing her harder and longer, helping her unbutton the rest of her blouse.

"Okay, you're right!" He pulls her blouse over her head, grabbing her tighter now, she slides onto his lap. They are breathing harder, lips locked, groping each other, and loving every single minute together.

"Okay, make it fast, I gotta go." Christy is a bit breathless.

"I don't do fast. I hope that's okay?" Daryl squeezes her tighter.

"I was hoping you would say that." Christy is smiling, she pulls her skirt up to her waist. Daryl is completely entranced. He absolutely respects Christy and is falling in love with her. He grins and reaches for the passenger door. Groping for the handle, he's not looking at it.

Christy is rubbing and pushing against him harder now.

Daryl barely catches the door handle, slamming it shut.

As they make love together.

13
BIG TIME OFFER

MIDLAND, TEXAS

Daryl stands in the rodeo arena with another bullfighter, Rob Bell, aged twenty-eight, spry and quick, he's good at this sport. There's a barrel man, Jose Martinez, aged thirty, who is dressed in rodeo clown garb and is making the crowd laugh, especially the kids, as he ducks in and out of his bullfighter barrel. Daryl and Rob are waiting for the bucking chute gate to open. The afternoon is nice and clear above them. The empty rodeo arena feels comfortable. Daryl has a look of experience now.

At least he holds a look of strong expectations as he climbs higher into the bullfighting world. He glances up toward the grandstands and focuses on Christy and Cody sitting about a dozen rows up. He lovingly waves at them, ready to fight the next bull. Daryl and Christy are spending their time together now full time as much as possible.

Bull and rider explode from the gate! Announcer gets

the large crowd's attention, they start cheering, as the massive bull starts bucking and twisting hard. Rob rushes forward and almost touches the big bull getting his attention. Daryl moves toward the bull from the other side, helping contain the animal in front of the bucking chutes. Jose moves a little closer and drops the barrel as a marker. The bull rider is twisting and turning with the huge bull in front of the bucking chutes...five seconds...six seconds...seven seconds...the bull rider is sticking on tight...eight seconds...the buzzer sounds loudly across the arena, the rider loses his seat and is ejected off the bull, but he cleared the time and scored.

The crowd are now clapping and cheering loudly, it was a nice ride. Rob steps in front of the bull, who suddenly turns and spins unexpectedly, smacking Rob hard in the side and throwing him several feet across the arena. The crowd gasps with surprise and shouts. Daryl darts forward, fighting the bull alone. Jose stands up inside the barrel, trying to keep the bull contained in one area. The beast turns and tries to get Daryl, who dodges and spins away, just barely escaping the bull's sharp horns.

Christy and Cody are watching with the crowd from the stands. Both have a look of concern on their faces, but Christy knows that Daryl is good at fighting bulls now. The two pickup men on horseback push the bad bull away toward the livestock exit gate. Daryl rushes over to Rob to help him to his feet. He starts to grab him, then realizes there's something hard poking out under his shirt near his lower ribs. The bull has broken a rib and it's protruding out like a stick! Rob's skin is wrapped around the rib under his shirt!

Daryl waves for the emergency techs who come into the arena with a stretcher and help Rob. Careful to not damage the broken rib any further. An ambulance backs up nearby outside the arena, the rodeo announcer standing above the arena floor calms the crowd, who are surprised and hopeful the injury is not too severe. Daryl helps raise Rob to his feet.

He looks up and waves at Christy, everything is okay. She is watching the injured bullfighter being strapped to the metal gurney and wheeled out of the arena. Rob is removed from the action, and the next bull rider is loading on top of a bigger, meaner-looking bull in the bucking chutes. Jose steps out of the barrel and joins Daryl in front of the chute gates. Daryl glances at him and nods, we got this. Jose nods his agreement.

Suddenly, the gate flies open! The next bull jumps from the bucking chute. He's twisting and trying to throw the bull rider, which he does in less than three seconds. The rider is slammed to the ground, the bull tries to hook him, but Daryl jumps in between and gets the bull chasing him. He runs to the arena fence and jumps on the rails, climbing to the top. Jose and the two pickup men on horseback are moving the mean bull away, as Daryl jumps back down and goes to the bull rider, making sure he's not hurt.

He helps him stand to his feet, the crowd is applauding their approval and giving thanks that he didn't get hurt. Daryl looks toward Christy and Cody, but they're not there, their seats are empty.

Daryl doesn't see them anywhere nearby.

———

DARYL SITS WITH CHRISTY AND CODY AT SMALL SQUARE table with four seats in the center of a local barbeque joint. Everyone is sharing fresh cheeseburgers and french fries. Cody is playing with a small rodeo clown figurine and a toy bull that Daryl bought him. He's making fighting noises like the bull is charging forward and beating up the rodeo clown. Christy listens for a few moments, then abruptly grabs his hand. "Baby, don't do that right now, I have a headache." Daryl takes a bite of his cheeseburger and glances over at her.

"You okay?" He's not sure what is bothering her.

Cody looks up at his mom; he's still tugging on the bull. "Why do you have a headache. Momma?" Christy stares back at him, she relaxes for a moment and releases his hand. She rubs the top of his fingers.

"I don't know, baby. Just too much going on today, I guess." Cody moves the bull toward the rodeo clown again, fighting, making more noises, Christy grabs his hand again.

"I said stop it!" She's obviously irritated, but Cody doesn't understand why.

"Daryl got these for me. They're fun to play with."

Christy jerks the toys out of Cody's hands and stuffs them into her purse. Daryl is watching her, not sure what to say. Cody is acting upset now. He turns away and folds his arms, not looking at his mother. He doesn't understand why his playing by himself is making her so mad. Christy offers a trade to settle him down a little. "How about some dessert? Want ice cream?" She tries to rub his back, but Cody pulls away.

"I wanna play." He still has his arms folded.

"I don't want you to play like that." Christy is serious.

Daryl looks at them both and tries to calm things down a little. "Hey, buddy, how about tomorrow we count the horns on the bulls. How'd you like that?"

"Don't tell him that." Christy is staring right at Daryl now.

"What's wrong with counting horns?"

"I'm not sure I want him around the bulls anymore." Christy looks upset.

"Why not? There's no danger in that." Daryl is a bit confused about where this is going.

"Everything is wrong with that!" Christy's voice level rises. "And nothing is right!" She stares over at Daryl. "Your friend got hurt today in the arena. His rib was sticking out of his body. And you act like it's no big deal." She watches him, obviously upset that it could have been Daryl. "We're all sitting here like it doesn't even matter!" She keeps staring at Daryl. Cody is looking up at her. Daryl gives her a moment.

"Rob is going to be fine. I called the hospital and spoke to him." He looks at Christy, trying to keep this as simple as possible. "Do you want to go to the hospital and see him?"

"I don't want to see you at the hospital!" She glares at him, then waves for the waitress, ready to pay and leave. Daryl doesn't want her upset, he puts his hand up at the waitress to hold off for another minute. The woman nods and turns away. Daryl looks at Christy and leans forward.

"I can't promise you I won't get hurt. It's part of the job." He watches her. Christy isn't happy.

"When my husband got hurt, we became obstacles. Things that got in his way." She's looking at Daryl, sincerity fills her voice. "I can't go through that again. Not ever."

Daryl watches her. He gives her a moment. Eyeing her closer. He needs to say this right. "Cody is about the same age that I was when my father got hurt and lost his chance to be a rodeo champion." He looks at them both Christy and Cody. "He went through the same thing. We all became objects. It changed his life." He watches Christy. Not looking away. "I know it's not the same thing, but…"

"But, what? Maybe you can replace Cody's father?" Christy is obviously more than upset, she's deeply concerned about Daryl possibly getting hurt and changing their love for each other.

"No, I didn't say that." Daryl feels bad she would imply that about him.

"Maybe you can be there for him when he cries himself to sleep, because he thinks that it's his fault his father left us. Or maybe explain to him why his father never calls him or his birthday or at Christmas."

"Christy, please…" Daryl is trying to keep their friendship together.

"I don't want this to be just a good time together. I want this to be a long-term relationship. I don't want to commit myself to something that can be over in a matter of moments." She stares right at Daryl. He can feel her hurt and disappointment from her previous relationship.

Daryl looks at her with genuine feelings, staring into her eyes, then glancing down at Cody. He really likes the boy and wouldn't mind helping raise him if that is what Christy wants. "I want this to last forever also." He's sincere and reaches for her hand, holding it tight, letting her know he's all in for the long ride. Cody hugs his mother, squeezing her with affection and love. "Momma, I like Daryl."

"I know, sweetie." Christy takes a breath and wipes some tears from her eyes. She smiles at Cody, then looks at Daryl who pinches her hand tighter. He leans forward and kisses her softly. Christy kisses him back; she really likes him a lot. More than that, she's also falling in love. Cody smiles and giggles. He likes it when they kiss each other. Christy takes another breath and exhales the bad air, she smiles. "I like him, too." She kisses Daryl back, holding it for a moment. Cody is very happy now. Hugging his mother tighter.

Christy feels Daryl is the right choice for her.

Daryl feels the same way.

IT'S A BRIGHT AND CLEAR AFTERNOON ON THE SECOND DAY inside the Midland rodeo arena. Daryl has just fought another dozen bulls. He comes walking out of the arena, bright rodeo clothes, his face painted red and white, his shirt is torn in the back where he almost got hooked. He looks satisfied that it was a good day keeping the bull riders safe.

He stuffs his silver necklace and the jeweled cross down into his shirt. Several of the bull riders and other cowboys congratulate him on a hard day's work. He shakes their hands and knuckle-bumps a few others. A man in his late forties, Javier Flores, average height and weight, with a big cowboy hat sitting over his head, approaches Daryl. He wears a nice suit jacket over his cowboy shirt, bolo tie, and blue jeans. "Hey Daryl, can you wait up a minute."

Daryl turns around and sees Javier. He's not familiar with him and doesn't know who he is. "How can I help you?" Daryl lets Javier approach him, as the other bull riders and contestants walk around them.

"I'm Javier Flores, the president of the ABR."

Daryl looks Javier over; he does look like an executive of sorts. "President of the American Bull Riders Association? That ABR?" Daryl waits for his answer. He sees Cody standing across the contestant area waiting for him and talking to a couple of calf ropers.

"Yes, that's right. You were pretty good out there today. Better than most that I've seen." Javier looks impressed with Daryl's work in the arena.

"Thanks, Mister Flores, I appreciate the accolades." Daryl is trying to be polite, still uncertain what Javier wants.

"How long you been doing this?" Javier watches him. Daryl stares back and grins.

"I suppose I'm still working off beginner's luck is all."

Javier steps a tad closer; he's a bit more serious now. "That's not what the bull riders are saying. They say you have real instincts, some of the best they've seen."

"Is this going somewhere, Mr. Flores?" Daryl is growing impatient. Cody is standing with the calf ropers.

"Please call me, Javier. And yes, maybe it's time you started fighting in some real competitions? The bigger rodeos, no more small stuff." Javier is watching him closer. Daryl waits a moment.

"You know that I'm a little older than most of these young hotshots, right?" Daryl looks at him.

"I don't care how old you are. We're looking to market new faces and new names. I'd like to sign you up with the American Bull Riders Association. What do you think?"

"As a professional bullfighter with the ABR?"

"Yep, you'll earn a chance to compete at the World Championships in Las Vegas at the end of the year. We hold them there every November." Daryl stares at him. It's a great offer.

"Is the pay any good?"

"Better than these regional rodeos."

Daryl looks at him a bit more serious now. The man in the suit jacket is making him a good offer. "If I accept, when do I start fighting for the ABR?"

"Next week at the show in Dallas. Then Houston, Denver, Phoenix. All the big cities."

"That's what you call them, shows? Daryl has a slight smile on his face.

"That's what they are. Shows." Javier is smiling now; he likes Daryl's attitude.

Daryl glances back across the contestant staging area. Cody is playing around and being wrangled by the calf ropers. They toss their lariats softly over his head. Daryl can't help but smile, he loves Cody's disposition about the rodeo world. "Can I take my girlfriend and her son. They'll be staying with me." He looks back at Javier. Not sure what to expect.

"Of course, we're family friendly." Javier sticks his hand out. Daryl looks at the open hand. Cody is laughing and playing with the steer ropers, having a good time. Daryl looks back at Javier and grabs his hand.

"Let's give it a try." He squeezes tight, Javier squeezes back. Then releases his hand.

"Terrific, welcome to the big leagues. We'll get a contract drafted and over to you by tomorrow. I'll get your email and phone number from the rodeo committee."

Daryl smiles at Javier and nods his approval. He looks back over at Cody who is throwing a lasso around one of the calf ropers. He's got him completely roped.

———

DARYL AND CHRISTY ARE ENJOYING A MEAL TOGETHER IN A nice restaurant with clean tables and white linens draped over the tops. Daryl is clean-shaven and paint free. Christy is cheerful and excited about Daryl's new job with the ABR. A male waiter, mid-thirties, handsome with a short, trimmed beard, pours them two glasses of white wine. He sets the bottle on the table. "Anything else for right now?"

"No, we're good." Christy picks up her glass, Daryl follows her lead. "Okay, then. Your dinner will be out soon enough. Enjoy the wine." The waiter turns and leaves them. Christy taps her glass against Daryl's. "Here's to our new professional bullfighter." She takes a sip.

Daryl sets his glass down and grabs his glass of water, taking a drink. "I can hardly believe it. I've only been fighting bulls for six months."

"You're good, Daryl. That's why the ABR wants you on their team."

She takes another sip of wine. Daryl watches her, smiling, he loves her more every day. He puts his water glass to his mouth to take another sip.

"So, what should I do with the wiener wagon?"

Daryl almost laughs and spits his water out on the table. "Take it with us of course. If you want to."

"They're not going to just let me plug into Cowboy Stadium and start selling hot dogs." She's laughing and smiling.

Daryl laughs with her and nearly chokes down his water. He coughs. "No, probably not." He smiles and leans over the table, kissing her. He watches her. "This is the first time I've taken something like this seriously." He's waiting for her reply.

"Are you talking about the professional bullfighting job—or us?" Christy smiles and kisses him back. She's falling for him more every day. Daryl reaches over the table and touches her hand.

"Both." Giving it a moment to set in with her. They stare at each other. He smiles again. "I'm falling in love with you, Christy. I hope you know that?"

"Wait another month until after you become a professional bullfighter. Then tell me that again." Christy is smiling wider now. She's excited and pleased.

"I'm going to start telling you that every day. That I love you." He kisses her passionately. Christy likes the attention. She kisses him back with genuine feelings.

They finally pull themselves away from each other. Almost laughing, they can't stay away from each other. The waiter approaches the table with their meals and sets them in front of each other. They wait until he leaves. Christy looks right at Daryl. "Let's make this work."

"With all my heart." Daryl smiles and nods at her.

Christy believes him.

14

THE BULLFIGHTER

ATT COWBOY'S STADIUM - DALLAS, TEXAS

DARYL AND TWO OTHER BULLFIGHTERS, CHET MILLER, aged twenty-eight, about Daryl's height and build, and Tate Burns, aged thirty-one, a little taller and wider, run out together into the giant rodeo arena thrown temporarily together on the football field at the Dallas Cowboy's home stadium. The stands are filled with enthusiastic rodeo spectators, all excited to be at this professional bull riding event. A camera follows and tracks them at ground level, with a camera operator on the high-definition mobile camera, and a first assistant operator helping with the lighting and sound, both running alongside the bullfighters.

The crowd cheers excitedly, the three bullfighters' images are shown on the giant big-screen hanging over the rodeo arena. The camera zooms in close on their faces, all painted different colors and wearing different outfits. Daryl wears his felt cowboy hat, Chet has a baseball hat pulled down on his head and turned backward, and Tate wears a straw hat with one side pinned back.

Daryl trots along with the two others toward the bucking chutes. Chet and Tate have been fighting for the ABR for a couple of years now. Daryl is absorbing the size and scope of the big time stadium. He rode in several larger rodeos but never rode bulls in a place this large. The ground under his feet is thicker than normal, the arena dirt is no less than six inches deep. He can feel the difference under his cleats.

Chet and Tate start jumping up and down in place, getting loosened up and getting ready to fight the bulls. Their warm-up is getting the crowd excited and ready. The spectators are shouting and cheering, ready for the action to start. Chet and Tate turn toward Daryl.

"You ever fight Spanish bulls?" Chet watches Daryl, who's stretching his legs a bit. "They're quick and fast. You can't make any mistakes with these dudes."

Tate jumps up and down again, loosening his neck and head side to side. "And they like to gore you."

"Who's in the barrel?" Daryl doesn't see a fourth bullfighter. There's a rodeo barrel planted in front of the bucking chutes, sitting by itself with another promotional logo wrapped around it.

"No one. Not tonight." Chet stretches his arms over his head. "We all need to stay out in front. There's two backup bullfighters if we need help." He motions to the other side of the arena, where Daryl sees two other bullfighters loosening up.

"Let's form a triangle around the bulls. I'll take the left side." Tate stretches his legs.

"I got the right side." Chet drops his arms to his side and shakes them out. Daryl is standing in front of the bucking chute. The rodeo barrel is sitting about ten feet behind them.

"Guess that means I'm straight up in front?" Daryl looks at the two other bullfighters, he's digging into the dirt, getting his comfortable stance.

Chet still standing close by, looking over at him. "These bulls like to move right and left as soon as they release, so don't worry, we'll be here to help." He starts digging his cleats into the dirt. Checking the depth.

Tate, also still nearby, is watching the bull in the chute behind the gate. He moves toward Daryl with one wide step. "We're not just fighting these bulls. We're also putting on a performance for the crowd."

"So, make it look good." Chet is now watching the chute gate as well. "It's all about the television ratings."

"And having a great time." Tate walks past Daryl and slaps some white talcum powder into his right hand. Daryl looks a little surprised. Tate and Chet peel off for the two sides. Daryl looks at the white talcum powder in his palm, he stares at it a moment. Then he grins and slaps his hands together. The white mist hangs in the air. The crowd reacts, cheering louder again. Daryl looks above the arena top railing and sees Christy and Cody sitting in the stands above him. They're about eight rows up behind the bucking chutes.

He waves at both. Cody lifts his hands and slaps them together, imitating Daryl. He makes a powder mist explosion around his face. Then smiles and waves at Daryl, who grins and laughs.

He looks around the huge stadium at the giant crowd sitting above him. It's almost surreal. He takes a deep breath and hunkers down. Chet and Tate are also ready and in place. Daryl looks at the bucking chute gate.

It bursts open!

The first bull rider explodes into the arena. He's riding a little black Spanish bull, that leaps and jumps all over the place. Twisting and spinning like a sixteen-hundred-pound ballerina on steroids. The bull gets into sight of Daryl standing in front of him and starts that way. Daryl is actually charging first toward the bull. He comes inside distracting the bull. Chet speeds in from the outside and now Tate. The three bullfighters start working the bull. Grabbing its attention, keeping it in one primary location. The bull rider on top is sticking hard on back...five seconds...six seconds...he slips and loses his seat, abruptly coming unglued, the little black bull tosses him into the dirt. The eight-second buzzer wails. No time.

Daryl gets to the bull first, dodging and weaving, but the Spanish bull is faster and suddenly scoops Daryl up by the pants and tosses him three feet into the air! Daryl lands on his feet and keeps moving, the crowd loves it, excitedly cheering and shouting. Christy is covering her eyes, but Cody is laughing and cheering loudly, cupping his hands around his mouth and shouting.

Tate dodges around the black beast. Chet runs past it, and now Daryl runs again toward the bull, tricking him into following him toward the livestock exit gate. He gets the bull almost there. The bull stops and stares at Daryl. Then charges right at him with its head down, horns coming fast. Daryl takes his fighting stance and squeezes his fist. Chet and Tate are coming over to help from the sides.

Daryl sprints right at the angry bull, meeting him headfirst. Daryl leaps over the black ball of angry fury and slaps him on the ass! White handprint marking the back of the bull! Daryl lands on his feet and turns looking at the white handprint mark he made. The crowd erupts into utter chaos and excitement. They haven't seen anything like that before. They roar their approval.

Chet and Tate cross again in front of the bull, whose head is still down. Surprised that the bullfighter touched him! The little black bull follows Daryl toward the live-stock exit gate. Daryl jumps up onto the arena fence rails. The black bull leaves the arena with the white handprint on his backside. The crowd is screaming loudly. No pickup men on horses. It's the bullfighters and their tenacious spirit only versus the wild bulls.

Daryl jumps off the fence rails back onto the arena floor. The big-screen overhead replaying in slow motion the moment that Daryl leaped over the bull and came down slapping him on the ass! Bright white handprint! Big letters light up the stadium boards flashing around the grandstands: SLAP THEM BULLS!

The crowd getting into the performance, loudly shouting. "Slap them bulls! Slap them bulls!" Chanting and yelling. Chet races over to Daryl and high-fives him. Talcum powder dusting them both.

"You're a big hit, man! Nice job!" He sprints back toward the bucking chutes.

Daryl stands there awestruck. He can't believe what he just did. Chet and Tate are waving at him. Come on back, we got more bulls to fight. Daryl is smiling and excited, he sees Christy and Cody standing in the crowd cheering with the other spectators. He runs back to his starting position.

Ready to fight more bulls.

————

THE BULLFIGHTING EVENT IS OVER. DARYL WALKS through the contestant area, several bull riders slapping him across the back. Congratulating him on a great job as he moves past them. They like his fighting style. A television crew is setting up to shoot the winning bull riders. Another camera team is following the Dallas Cowboy's owner, Jerry Jones, who also walks through the contestant area, he enthusiastically approaches Daryl and throws his hand out.

"Slap them bulls!" He grins wide and the television crew lights up Daryl's painted face. He looks back at Jerry, then teasingly slaps his open hand. White talcum powder mist explodes around them. Jerry is all smiles. He shows the television cameras his white hand. He high-fives Daryl with the same hand and moves toward the top bull riders to congratulate them. The contestants all cheer and shout their approval.

Daryl is grinning, as Chet and Tate approach him, they are impressed with his ability to fight the bulls. The three bullfighters are standing together. Television cameras quickly pick up shots of them and a sports reporter starts asking them questions and getting good answers. Daryl can't believe he's in the big leagues now with the ABR. Christy and Cody come walking into the contestant area and watch the television crew interviewing the three bullfighters and some of the bull riders. Daryl is one of the main attractions. He notices his new family standing across the floor and waves at them.

Liking every minute.

———

DARYL STANDS SHIRTLESS IN FRONT OF THE MIRROR IN THE bathroom in his hotel room. He's come a long way in a short period of time since his wreck in San Angelo seven months earlier. He touches the scar on his cheekbone which is very visible in the bathroom light. Suddenly, he has a flashback of the big bull in San Angelo smashing his head into his face. Daryl exhales and collects himself.

He checks his ribs. They're scarred where the surgeons had to repair the damage. He remembers the bull landing on his ribs. He remembers the cracking and sheer pain, and his scream of terror and hurt.

Darl presses against his chest, he slightly winces. There's still some discomfort and pain renewed by the new bullfighting. He dumps his toiletry kit onto the bathroom sink counter looking for something to help with the discomfort. An old bottle of prescription pills drops into the sink. Daryl picks up the bottle and looks at the prescription label. Knock on the bathroom door. Daryl glances over and tosses the prescription pills into the trash can under the sink. He opens the door, and Christy is standing there in some very sexy lingerie. She holds an open bottle of champagne and two plastic glasses, noticing the scars on his ribs and face in the bathroom light.

"Hey Cowboy, the kid is out for the night." She smiles at Daryl, who grins and steps toward her, kissing her. Daryl grabs the bottle of champagne and sets it on the vanity outside the door, sweeping Christy toward the bed. She giggles and drops on top of the bedspread with him, still holding the plastic cups, kissing him passionately. "I guess we don't need these." She tosses the cups on the other side of the bed. Daryl is on top of her, they start groping at each other. Kissing passionately again.

The two-way door between Daryl's room and the

room next door is closed shut but unlocked. Christy pulls her lingerie off over her head. Daryl is in seventh heaven again. He begins to kiss her neck and body, making her feel good and loved. She strokes his shoulders and arms. Gently dropping down and lying underneath him. Rubbing herself against the man she loves. She wants this to be part of her life for a long time.

DARYL AND CHRISTY LAY SLEEPING IN BED TOGETHER IN the same hotel room as the night before. Daryl stirs and jerks in his sleep, waking Christy. She moves closer to him and comforts him, holding him in her arms. She glances at the digital clock on the nightstand, the red numbers showing six-thirty a.m. She snuggles even closer and feels the newer scars on his chest. She quietly traces the outlines of the injuries, showing that she cares for him.

There are several other older scars on his body that she finds, a track record of his past accomplishments and disappointments. She likes lying with him close like this in bed together. Daryl slowly wakes up and realizes Christy is right next to him, he turns his head and lovingly kisses her. "Good morning..."

"Morning, handsome."

Daryl's eyes are still closed as he softly kisses her again and strokes her hair back from her face, while she traces his damaged ribs. "I've been thinking. 'Slap Them Bulls' would make a great trademark and logo. We could add a little handprint and put it on merchandise like T-shirts and other things." She squeezes him a little tighter, then pulls her hand off his chest. "We should set this up and do it before someone else comes up with the idea. It could make money."

Daryl is looking at her now, swiping her hair aside again. He kisses her one more time. "You really think so?"

Christy raises herself up a little, softly rubbing his side under the sheets. "We could put it on social media and get you some big-name exposure. The more attention you get, the more the ABR might want to have you at all the bigger events. Even the World Championships."

"Exposure?" Daryl slides himself up a little on his pillow.

"Like I said, start marketing you with T-shirts, cups, glasses, koozies, posters, and even billboards." She's totally into the idea. "This could be huge."

"Billboards, huh?" He rubs her bottom under the sheets. Christy laughs and pushes his hand away.

"We need to build you a fan base. Let them know what you're all about. What you can do for the sport."

"Maybe I don't want them to know what I'm all about," he teases her then starts kissing her. Christy likes it but now is not the time.

"Do you want to get to the bullfighting World Championships or not?"

Daryl looks at her, he's smiling. It's a bit early to be thinking like this that far ahead. "Yeah, but beer koozies, really?" He laughs and kisses her again. She kisses him back and then pulls away.

"You'll be wrapped around every beer bottle and soda pop can in America. Have a drink with Daryl Weathers, the famous bullfighter. Slap them bulls!" She's smiling now. Daryl stares at her, he thinks it's a crazy plan, but he likes it. However, he's a bit embarrassed and not sure this would really work. People might think he's a joke. Christy thinks it's a great plan. "Let's do this."

The door between the rooms swings open!

Cody dressed in his light blue pajamas, rushes toward the bed. He jumps on top of them. "What are you guys talking about in here?!"

Christy makes sure she is covered with the sheet and grabs him, tickling him. Daryl starts doing the same. "We're talking about you, munchkin!" Christy kisses him on top of the head. Daryl pinches him on the sides. Cody is wiggling and squealing with delight.

"What did I do?" Cody is giggling harder.

"Nothing!" Daryl pinches him harder. Cody loves it.

"That's the problem!" Christy tickles him some more, as Daryl grabs Cody and lifts him over his head, Christy pulling the sheets close to her and watching. Smiling and enjoying the closeness of the three of them together. Cody is laughing louder and squealing with delight. Christy watches her beautiful son enjoying time with her new man. His new father figure.

She wants this to last forever.

————

BROADMOOR ARENA - COLORADO SPRINGS, COLORADO

Daryl stands in his bullfighting position in another large rodeo arena in front of the bucking chutes. Chet and Tate are standing off to the sides ready to fight the next bull. The three bullfighters have been touring together for the past several weeks. There's a large sign over the stadium "Broadmoor Arena, Colorado Springs." The large crowd is boisterous and jacked up tonight.

Daryl has a small pouch tied to his hip that is filled with white talcum powder. His hands are already coated with powder. He reaches inside the bag and grabs a handful of the white powder and slaps his hands together in front of himself. His palms explode with a vibrant white mist floating through the arena. The crowd goes viral. Cheering and shouting as loud as possible. "Slap them bulls! Slap them bulls!" They chant in unison, their voices filling the stadium. Daryl is grinning and almost laughing at how this has become so popular. Chet and Tate are both giving him a thumbs-up.

The chute gate bursts open and a large Brahma bull and young rider, about age twenty-six, wearing a safety helmet and face mask, blow into the arena. Chet comes rushing in from one side and Tate runs in from the other. Daryl is staying in the middle, waiting a few moments, then moving toward the bull...four seconds... five seconds...the bull twists and turns, trying to shake off the rider with the helmet. The three bullfighters surround the beast, six seconds...seven seconds...the bull quickly spins around...eight seconds...the arena buzzer sounds, the rider has scored, he leaps free and hits the dirt.

The bull turns toward him. Daryl is there first, waving his arms and dodging around the angry bundle of thunder, as Chet and Tate take turns distracting him. Chet comes back in from the right side, the bull swiftly turning, lowering its head and starts to move into Chet, as Daryl comes in and slaps the bull on the ass! Talcum powder blast fills the arena. White handprint stuck in the bull's backside.

The beast spins around away from Chet, toward Daryl. The crowd is frenzied, cheering loudly and screaming. The giant overhead big-screen showing the action around the arena. Tate rushes between Daryl and the angry bull. The animal is chasing him toward the livestock exit gate. Tate jumps on the arena fence. The bull runs out of the arena through the gate.

Daryl and Chet are looking at each other, both catching their breath, both wearing huge grins. Tate drops off the fence and is jogging back toward them. The crowd is chanting again, "Slap them bulls! Slap them bulls!" The words displayed in big letters moving across the large, big-screen boards surrounding the arena. Daryl is trying to show composure. He's completely absorbed in his new world.

"Slap Them Bulls" is a hit.

15
RISING STAR

Rodeo music is playing over a series of shots of Daryl fighting bulls in various rodeo arenas around the West. He dodges, sidesteps, jumps, leaps, flies, twists, turns, and slaps various bulls on the back ends with his white talcum powder handprints. There are a few narrow escapes and a few knockdowns, but he always gets back up and keeps fighting.

Daryl is the rising star of his professional sport. Now he's doing interviews with sports reporters for various sports channels, there are camera crews and photographers. Daryl can't believe all his luck, he's just along for the ride, doing what he feels is best. He sees Rex at one rodeo event and tries to ignore him, other than keeping him safe in the arena when he rides his bulls. Rex throws Daryl a cold look after a couple strong rides, he doesn't want Daryl near his bulls.

Christy and Cody attend all the rodeos. Christy is selling T-shirts and hot dogs at her vendor booth. Cody is selling beer and soda koozies and Daryl's autograph to adults and kids alike. There are several vendors now selling Daryl's likeness and the white handprint on T-shirts, cups and glasses, posters, and beach towels!

Daryl is autographing more posters. He's autographing body parts on both cowboys and cowgirls. Christy watches him autograph the cowgirls and teases Daryl that she wants one under her blouse. Daryl grins wide, there's plenty of smiles, kissing and real bonding between Daryl, Christy, and Cody. Daryl is now doing talcum powder high fives for five dollars per slap. He does a talcum powder sports commercial for the ABR, slapping a couple of pretty cowgirls on the back of their tight-fitting jeans. The commercial is a huge hit on the internet.

More bullfighting. Daryl is chasing angry bulls, slapping them on the back end. More bull riders thanking Daryl for keeping them safe.

Christy and Cody jump on top of a large king bed in a hotel room, both wearing Daryl's "Slap Them Bulls!" T-shirts. Both are throwing cash into the air!

Daryl is standing with his arms crossed with several other bullfighters taking photos together. Chet and Tate are standing on each side of him with their arms crossed. The bullfighters look threatening, a force to be reckoned with. Cody steps in next to the group and crosses his arms, looking every part as confident as the other bullfighters. Daryl has to smile.

Rex stands across the contestant area outside the arena. He sees Daryl kissing Christy and hugging Cody. He thinks it's all a farce, that Daryl is taking advantage of Christy and their relationship won't last. He's not happy about it. He told Christy, but she told him to quit worrying. Daryl is a changed man.

Rex doesn't believe her.

NATIONAL WESTERN COMPLEX - DENVER, COLORADO

Daryl has his arm around Christy, who holds Cody's hand, as they all walk together toward the security gate entrance outside the huge National Western Rodeo Complex in Denver, Colorado. This is where the National Western Stock Show is held every January and where the Rodeo All-star Event is being held now in early October. They reach the security gate. There's a large, heavily built security guard in full uniform at the entrance. He weighs no less than two hundred and fifty pounds.

Suddenly, Rory walks up behind them. "Daryl! Wait up!"

Daryl turns to see Rory standing there. He's completely surprised to see him in Denver. Actually, he's completely surprised to see him at all. They haven't spoken in several months, since Daryl started fighting bulls in the big leagues. Christy and Cody turn and look at Rory as well.

"Rory? What the heck are you doing here?" He grabs Rory in a tight hug and slaps him across both shoulders. "You should have called!"

Rory is all smiles. "I tried. Several times. You never pick up your phone anymore." Rory is looking at Daryl.

"It's really been crazy lately. Sorry about that." He looks behind Rory. "Where's Sarah Jane and the girls?"

"Back home. They couldn't make it."

"Are you staying for the show?"

"That's what you call it now? A show?" Rory laughs. He looks at Christy and Cody. "So, ya gonna introduce me to this beautiful woman and handsome boy?" He's grinning.

"Of course." Daryl puts his arm around him and turns to face Christy and Cody. "Rory, this is Christy, my new girlfriend, and her son, Cody. They've been with me about three months now."

"Wow, you're a lucky man. She's gorgeous." He squeezes Christy in a friendly hug, then releases her. He looks at Cody and fist-bumps him. "Hey, buddy…" Rory turns and looks at Daryl, his facial expression abruptly turns serious. "I need your help, Daryl. I rode with you for almost ten years. I need a big favor." He's looking straight at Daryl, who can see there's a possible problem here.

"What do you need? I'd like to help you." Daryl isn't sure what Rory is going to ask.

"I'm dead broke, Daryl." He looks at Daryl in earnest, waiting a moment. Christy and Cody are watching, not sure where this is going. "I'm not riding bulls anymore. It's been hard to find work."

"I paid you everything back." Daryl is watching him.

"It's not about the money." He takes a short breath. "We lost our home. The bank foreclosed on us."

Daryl is looking at him.

"Sarah, and the girls, we all need a new place to live…" He watches Daryl. "I was hoping you'd let us move on to the ranch?"

Daryl waits a moment, looking at Rory. "That's Tommy's place. Not mine. You know that."

"Half the ranch is yours. I know your daddy left it for you. Tommy told me. We just need a couple acres that we can set a mobile home on temporarily, until I get regular work." He's watching Daryl, his eyes almost pleading for help. "It's for Sarah and the girls, Daryl." They stare at each other.

The large security guard approaches them. He's wearing a taser gun on his belt with handcuffs. "Everything okay here, Mr. Weathers?" Looking at Rory with a suspicious expression. "They're waiting for you inside." He sizes Rory up and down now, gauging what he really wants. Daryl sees the real honesty in Rory's eyes and face. He looks at the security guard.

"Yeah, we're fine. This is one of my best friends. Can you radio the arena crew that we'll be inside in a few minutes. I'd appreciate that."

The security guard looks at Rory one more time, then nods his understanding. "Yes, sir." Taking another look at Rory, he turns and goes back to his booth at the security entrance and gets on the radio to the other security personnel.

"Tommy won't speak to me since our daddy died. He still blames it on me." Daryl is watching Rory, who touches Daryl on the shoulder.

"He knows it wasn't your fault. Your dad's heart was going bad. He's just gotta know that you said yes about moving the mobile home onto the ranch." Rory's trying to remain calm, Daryl glances over at Christy. She offers a nice smile and nods her head.

Daryl pulls Rory aside so Christy and Cody can't hear them. "I want to help." Rory's expression changes to a wide smile, and he hugs Daryl, who squeezes him back. Christy and Cody are watching. Daryl looks at Christy, she's got her arm wrapped around Cody. "I'm in love with her, Rory. I might even ask her to marry me." He looks back at Rory. "Maybe you can be my best man?" He grins again. Rory is smiling, feeling relieved. Daryl is still a true friend. He looks straight at Daryl.

"Does she know that yet?" Rory smiles wider.

"Not yet." Daryl is grinning and feeling good. He grabs Rory's hand and squeezes hard. "Thanks for being there for me when I needed you. I'll never forget that." He's watching Rory a little closer with a genuine and sincere look. "Tell Tommy, I said 'yes.' Get your family moved onto the ranch."

Rory squeezes his hand back tighter. Excitement is building in his face. "Thank you, Daryl. You're still a good man." He grabs Daryl in a hug one more time, then releases him, holding his happy smile.

"You gonna stay and watch me fight some bulls? I can get you a seat." Daryl grins at him.

"Hell, yes! I didn't come all this way to not watch the 'show.'" Rory high-fives him. "Slap them bulls, baby! You're the hottest ticket in town!" Daryl grins deeper. They both laugh together. They move toward Christy and Cody. Going through the security gate entrance.

———

DARYL, CHRISTY, AND CODY ARE WASHING DOWN THE wiener wagon outside a local hotel in the parking lot. They wipe and wash the hot dog stand with soap and water, having fun together. Playing and teasing one another with the water hose and two buckets of soap and bubbles.

There's a portable boombox plugged in outside with music playing loud. Moe Bandy's popular hit rodeo song *"Bandy the Rodeo Clown,"* is playing over the speaker:

"...who was once a bull-hooking son of a gun, now who keeps a pint hid out behind chute number one..."

Daryl and Cody soap down the trailer together, they're laughing and trying to overlap each other's hands with the wet rags. Christy rinses the soap suds off behind them, then turns the hose on them both, spraying them with water. Cody is squealing with delight, Daryl laughing harder, trying to get the hose from Christy now. Moe Bandy's song continues over the action:

"...who was riding high till a pretty girl rode him to the ground, any kid knows where to find me, I'm Bandy the rodeo clown..."

Daryl finally grabs the hose from Christy and turns it around on her, spraying her over the head. She throws her hands up, trying to block the water from hitting her and laughing as hard as the two others. It's a delightful moment between them all, everyone is soaking wet. They're having more fun than work, the laughter and playfulness filling the air over the music.

Moe Bandy's song fades off the speakers, just as Daryl's cell phone buzzes in his back pocket. Christy has the hose again and sprays toward him. Daryl grabs his phone, dodging the stream of water, laughing and chiding her to stop, he's got to answer his phone. He steps further away out of range of the spray hose, smiling and wiping his face off. He looks at his cell phone but doesn't recognize the number on the screen.

"This is Daryl," answering the call and catching his breath.

"Daryl, it's Javier Flores at the ABR in Pueblo. How are you doing?"

Daryl is a bit surprised; he watches Cody trying to wrestle the water hose away from his mother. They're laughing and playing together. "Mr. Flores? What a nice surprise. We're all doing fine. How are you?" Christy is trying to not get sprayed by Cody, she ducks behind the wiener wagon. Daryl is grinning.

Javier sits in a swivel chair at his desk at the American Bull Riders Association main offices in Pueblo, Colorado. The office has windows on one side and is clean and immaculate, everything organized and in order. The same cowboy hat with expensive silver hatband that he met Daryl in when he first spoke to him, hangs on a coat rack with a Western vest near the office door. "Where are you right now?" Javier has his portable office phone in his hand and is glancing at some paperwork in a folder laying on his desk.

Daryl looks toward the wiener wagon. Christy is hiding behind the back end. Cody is trying to pull the water hose that way, but there's no more length to go that far. "On our way to the Phoenix semi-finals. Are you flying in for the rodeo?" Daryl watches Cody trying to untangle a knot in the water hose. Christy runs around the other side of the hot dog booth to sneak up in him.

Javier swivels his office chair around toward the wide glass windows. The majestic Rocky Mountains rise in the near distance, their high peaks capped with a touch of early snowfall. "I'm gonna miss it. We're getting ready for the World Championships next month in Las Vegas." He glances back at the paperwork in front of him on his desk.

"Wish I could be there, sounds like a great event." He's watching Christy and Cody playing with the water hose again. "Maybe next year, huh?"

"I wanted to talk to you about that." Javier flips the paper on his desk over and tucks it under another paper below it. It's a professional photo of Daryl fighting a massive bull. "You've done a great job for our organization, Daryl. And we want to thank you for that." Lifting the photograph up to eye level. He gauges the bullfighter. "Slap Them Bulls! It's pure marketing genius." Javier has a smile on his face.

"That was Christy's idea." He watches Christy turn the hose off, wet and beautiful. She swipes her hair from her face, the morning sun glowing softly around her. "I'm lucky she thought of it."

"You got raw talent, Daryl. You're definitely a natural bullfighter. Something we don't see a lot in this sport."

"It's hard to mess up bullfighting when there's no instruction manual." He grins and looks toward the motel parking lot. Here's several trucks and stock trailers parked there. "It's always different every time. Never the same. Except the attitude of the bulls, that doesn't change." He laughs at his remark. Javier laughs on his phone. He sets Daryl's photo down.

"Actually, Daryl. We all think you can do a lot better."

Daryl turns and looks at Christy, who is walking toward him. He looks at her lovely face, she can see there's something not sitting right from the expression on his face. Daryl isn't sure what Javier is talking about. Javier leans forward over his desk. He pulls another photograph from the other side of the work pile. It's a promotional marketing layout with a picture of several ABR bullfighters, the "best of the best."

Daryl's photo is right in the middle of the page in the foreground. The title on the promotional marketing piece says: 'World's Best Bullfighters.'

"The reason that I'm calling you today, Daryl, is that we want you to represent the ABR in the World Championships in Las Vegas next month. We've chosen you and four other bullfighters. Two will be backup bullfighters. You and two others will compete for the top honor as the world's best bullfighter."

Daryl stands there for a moment, not sure what he just heard. Christy is only a few feet away watching him. Cody is still trying to untangle the water hose. Daryl looks at Christy, speaking into his cell phone to Javier. "Are you sure about this? Did I hear you correctly?"

"We're inviting you to the World Championships this year." Daryl stares at Christy, his expression is starting to become one of joyful happiness. "Do you want to join us there? I hope you do."

"Heck, yes!" Daryl almost screams his answer into the cell phone. He looks back at Christy with a big smile on his face. She responds with her wonderful smile. "Are you sure about this?" Looking right at Christy.

"We couldn't be surer of it." Javier sets the promotional flyer down on his desk. "I'll send you all the details. Thank you again for the great job." He hangs up the phone.

Daryl stares at Christy. He clicks off his cell phone and steps toward her.

"What was that all about?"

"We got a problem." Daryl looks at her face.

"What problem?" Christy is looking right back at him.

"That was Javier Flores from the ABR. He wants me to go to Las Vegas."

"What? When?" Christy is trying to put it together. Cody walks up to them.

"As soon as Phoenix is over." He looks at them both. Now a huge smile wrapping around his grin. "I'm competing for the World Championships in Las Vegas!"

Christy stares at him, then grabs him tight. "I knew you would make it!" She kisses him. Daryl holds her tight.

"You're a badass, Daryl!" Cody steps forward to knuckle bump him. Daryl knuckle-bumps him back.

"Hey, watch your language, mister." Christy looks down at Cody, he's smiling. She looks back at Daryl, then smiles and laughs. "Okay, you're right, he is a badass!" She grabs Daryl closer, wrapping her other arm around Cody and pulling him close to them as one family.

"Badass! Badass!" Cody is enjoying the closeness.

Daryl is grinning wide, enjoying the love of both of them. He ruffles Cody's hair on his head. "Let's go finish washing the wiener wagon."

"I got the hose! Beat you there!" Cody peels away to turn on the water.

Christy looks at Daryl. She's very happy right now. "Thank you for being so good with him."

"I love you." Daryl leans forward and kisses her with emotion. Christy pulls away.

"I love you, too." She kisses him back with the same passion. Holding it for a long moment. Then releasing him. Her loving smile is worth a thousand words.

16
WEDDING VOWS

THE STRIP—LAS VEGAS, NEVADA

IT'S A BEAUTIFUL CLEAR NIGHT WITH STARRY SKIES AND A partial moon hanging overhead above the glitz and glamour of Las Vegas, Nevada. Thousands of glittering lights and neon signs from the high-rise hotels filling the six and eight-lane strip boulevard through the center of town. There's enough neon lighting to make it almost feel like daylight.

Daryl drives Christy's newer pickup truck through the gauntlet of lights. The hot dog vending wiener wagon booth has been left in Phoenix. They both stare at the bright colored lights reflecting off the front windshield. Cody sleeps in the back seat, and the day for night feeling in this desert oasis almost overwhelms them. Even now during the winter months.

"So many lights..." Christy is almost mesmerized by the power of the neon lights.

"So many hopes..." Daryl is thinking of all the bull riders and other rodeo performers that have come to the ABR World Championships, and the Professional Rodeo Cowboys Association's National Finals Rodeo held the following month in December in this same tourist city. The bright lights keep sweeping past them. Daryl goes quiet now, watching the famous strip boulevard.

"What are you thinking?" Christy is a little breathless at the enormous size and scope of the thousands of lights. She's never been to Las Vegas. Her brother Rex has been here many times.

"My daddy wanted to come here and ride bulls. He felt it was his destiny." He's quiet for a moment. "And now I'm here. Fighting them." The irony of it all is a bit unique and surreal. Daryl almost feels a little remorse that his father was on his way to the World Championships when it was taken from him in a matter of moments in the bad bull wreck that he watched as a kid. "I wish he was here with us. I'd feel a lot better."

"Maybe he is." Christy is looking at him. She grabs his arm, offering reassurance. "He's probably watching you right now. Proud that his son has made it to the top of the rodeo world." She smiles warmly at him. Daryl looks at her for a moment. Then, breaking into a smile, he nods his agreement. He likes her thinking. As they sweep past several more high-rise hotels and casinos lit up like the Fourth of July.

DARYL PULLS CHRISTY'S PICKUP TRUCK INTO THE PARKING lot of the South Point Hotel & Casino. It's a large resort on the south end of the Las Vegas Strip with a hotel, casino, rodeo arena, pool and spa. It's a popular spot for rodeo cowboys and cowgirls. There are several pickup and semi-trucks in the huge five-acre asphalt open parking lot with large horse trailers attached.

Many of the trailers have sleeping quarters and can carry four to six horses. One of the bigger semi-trucks has a giant trailer attached to move bulls from rodeo to rodeo. Daryl recognizes it from some of the other ABR rodeos he's fought at.

He stares at the wide six-door hotel entrance across the parking lot. They are actually only about two hundred feet away from the main entrance. The neon lights in front of the hotel and casino fill the truck cab with a golden glow. It's almost like a dream. Cody is still sleeping in the back seat; he hasn't moved yet.

Daryl watches the cowboys and cowgirls going in and out of the main hotel entrance. Christy is watching as well, absorbing all the activity. Daryl puts a new smile on his face. He glances at Christy, then reaches into the left pocket of his rodeo logo blazer jacket and pulls out a small box. The size of an engagement ring box. Christy turns her head and looks at Daryl, she sees the small box. "I got something for you." Daryl opens the lid on the box; there's a beautiful engagement ring and wedding band sitting inside. He puts the box in front of Christy. His hopes are swirling high over his head, his face lit up and glowing.

"Will you marry me?"

Christy is taken by complete surprise, she knew they cared for each other deeply, their relationship has been getting more comfortable and closer. But she wasn't expecting this now. Not when Daryl is getting ready to compete for the World Bullfighting Championships! She stares at the engagement ring and wedding band. Looking back at Daryl. "What?"

"Marry me. Tonight. There's a little white church off

the Vegas strip that they always show on television. I looked it up online. Everyone's welcome at any time. No appointments."

Christy stares at him. "Daryl...this is so sudden. We didn't even plan it with our families."

"Does it matter?" He watches her. "I love you more than anything else. I want to be with you forever."

Cody stirs in the back seat and suddenly wakes up, opening his eyes. The bright neon hotel and casino lights glowing in his face. He partially shields his eyes with his forearm. "Momma? Are we in Las Vegas?"

Christy smiles and looks over the front seat into the back seat of the truck. "Yes, baby. We're here." She looks at Daryl again, a big smile on her face. He waits patiently. "This is a big step."

"I know. But I want to be with you and Cody. It's my destiny."

Christy is still looking at him with her wonderful smile. "Cody...Daryl just asked me to marry him. What do you think about that? You okay with him being your new daddy?"

"Marry you?" He's still waking. He sits up and leans closer to the front seat. "He'll really be my new daddy?"

"If you want him to be." Christy is looking at Daryl again.

"That would be nice." Cody is leaning closer.

"Are you sure?" Christy rubs his head.

"Yep. I'm sure." Cody is still yawning and waking.

Christy stares at Daryl again, she's got a bright smile on his face now as well. "Yes. I will. Marry you."

"I love you." Daryl leans toward her and kisses her. Right in front of Cody.

"I love you, too." Christy finds his lips and kisses him back, enjoying her new husband-to-be. Cody is grinning in the back seat right next to them. They kiss again and he covers his eyes, then smiles and peeks through his fingers. He puts his arms around them both.

"I love you guys, too."

All laughing and hugging each other.

———

DARYL STANDS WITH CHRISTY IN A LITTLE WHITE WEDDING chapel with about a dozen rows of seats. There's a nice audience of cowboys and cowgirls from the rodeo World Championships there to witness the ceremony. It's the perfect addition to being in Las Vegas. Getting married. Christy wears a simple white wedding veil on top of her head. She's dressed in a nice comfortable cowgirl dress. It's not white, there wasn't time to buy a wedding gown.

Cody stands next to Daryl, substituting for Rory as best man. Rory and his wife Sarah Jane and their two daughters are watching the wedding ceremony on Daryl's cell phone. The screen propped up at the altar with a perfect view of the happy couple. A pretty barrel racer, Collete, aged thirty, is the bridesmaid for Christy. Several cowgirls at the South Point Hotel picked the long end of their straws and Collette won the honor. Four bull riders and two bullfighters competing against Daryl in the World Championships stand on the other side of Cody as the other best men.

All the cowboys are dressed in their finest cowboy clothes, wearing their clean cowboy hats, polished boots and belt buckles, and nice frock coats. Three other cowgirls, the wives of some of the bull riders, are standing on the other side of Collette as bridesmaids in their pretty evening dresses.

A minister of all faiths, Reverend Michaels, late

sixties, with gray hair and a short-cropped gray beard, is standing between Daryl and Christy. He delivers the opening of their wedding vows, keeping it short and sweet. "Daryl, do you take this lovely woman, Christy, to be your wonderful wife?"

"Yes, sir. I do." He's staring right into Christy's eyes.

"And Christy, do you take this handsome man, Daryl, to be your loving husband?"

Christy's smile is all-absorbing. "Yes, sir. I certainly do."

The presumable minister smiles at them both. He pauses for a moment and looks down at Cody, offering a light whisper. "Do you have your mother's wedding ring?" Cody nods he does and hands the ring to the minister, who hands it over to Daryl. "Go ahead and put the wedding ring on her finger." Daryl has a wide smile and slips the wedding band over Christy's left finger.

The reverend watches for a moment with a sincere approval and then continues. "Therefore, under the laws set forth by the statutes of Clark County, State of Nevada. I now bound you as husband and wife from this moment forward. You may kiss the bride."

"Kiss her! Kiss her!" The bull riders and bullfighters are encouraging Daryl to seal the deal. "Kiss her!" Rory and his wife are shouting through the cell phone. Their two daughters are giggling and laughing. Cody joins the others in the room. "Kiss her!" He's smiling and pushing Daryl toward his mother. Daryl doesn't need to hear it again. He leans forward and passionately kisses Christy, completely excited to have her in his life forever. Christy passionately returns the wedding kiss.

The bridesmaids are excited and encouraging. Collette says it best, "You go, girl!" The small audience in the open chapel are also clapping their approval and cheering. Daryl and Christy pull their lips apart, laughing together. They both turn and look at their guests. The minister stands between them and just behind.

"Ladies and gentlemen...may I present, Mr. Daryl Weathers and Mrs. Christy Weathers."

More whooping and hollering.

Cody steps forward and hugs his mother. He high-fives Daryl.

The bull riders and bullfighters now congratulate Daryl, slapping him across the shoulders, shaking his hand, letting him know he's a very lucky man. Rory has his hands clamped around his mouth and is hooraying through the cell phone. "Way to go, Daryl!"

The bridesmaids offer Christy emotional support and genuine approval. Collette smiles at her, then takes her hand and looks at the wedding ring. "Absolutely gorgeous." She offers a heartfelt hug as Christy squeezes her back. She turns to Daryl; their eyes locked on each other.

"You're so beautiful." Daryl is completely in love.

"Thank you." Christy feels the same.

"I truly do love you." Daryl kisses her again. Christy kisses him back. Daryl is all smiles.

"That's the best part." Christy kisses him deeper.

They pull away and laugh. Looking at the guests. The groomsmen and bridesmaids whooping and hollering. Cody feels like a million bucks.

A bottle of champagne is popped. And now another one, and several more bottles, lose their tops, as two full glasses of champagne are being shoved into Daryl and Christy's hands.

They toast each other and take a sip. Daryl hasn't drunk alcohol in over eight months. It tastes strange, so he just sips on the champagne to seal the wedding vows.

Two other kids about Cody's age, a girl and a boy, appear and hand him an open soda pop can. Cody laughs and taps his soda can against theirs. They all toast the happy couple.

Let the party begin.

17
WORLD CHAMPIONSHIPS!

T-MOBILE ARENA—LAS VEGAS, NEVADA

IT'S A PACKED HOUSE. THE TWENTY THOUSAND SEATS IN the T-Mobile indoor arena are filled to maximum capacity with eager rodeo fans. All waiting for the American Bull Riders Association's World Championships Bull Riding and Bullfighting competition to start. The noise and excitement are drowning out regular conversations.

Christy and Cody sit in the arena seats below the announcer's booth. They are standing and dancing to the music and lyrics of country music singer Clay Walker's song *"Long Live the Cowboy"* playing over the loudspeakers, much like the rest of the audience. Daryl runs into the rodeo arena down below dressed in his bullfighting outfit with his felt cowboy hat, colorful wardrobe and bull rags, and football cleats. His face is painted red, white, and blue! He's followed by two other bullfighters, Blake Hayes, aged 30, lean and mean, with a straw cowboy hat on his head, and Bobby Morrow, aged twenty-nine, blond hair and blue eyes. He wears a base-ball cap backward.

There's a bullfighter barrel in the arena, but no barrel man. The crowd erupts with loud cheers and shouts as the bullfighters move toward the bucking chutes. Clay Walker's song drops away. The crowd is cheering louder. Several are whistling their approval. Loud and straight-forward.

Christy and Cody are clapping and cheering with the audience. Cody sticks his fingers into his mouth and tries to whistle. Nothing comes out except an exhale of air. Christy grins at him and sticks two of her fingers into her mouth. Blowing long and hard, it's a beautiful and loud, shrieking whistle! Cody is completely surprised; he's never seen his mother whistle like that!

Daryl stands in the middle of the three rodeo bull-fighters. They take their starting positions. Blake on the left and Bobby on the right. Daryl starts digging into the soft soil, preparing for a great event. He's completely embodied in this surreal moment of enthusiasm and gratitude. He feels so lucky to have gotten his life together and married a wonderful woman with a great son. He now has a family of his own.

The bucking chutes are being loaded with several massive bulls, some of the biggest and meanest in the rodeo world. The crowd is watching and clapping and cheering louder now, they are ready to get this show started.

Daryl takes a deep breath and glances toward the top rafters of the indoor stadium, grabbing the silver neck-lace and jeweled cross around his neck. He kisses the cross and holds it high toward the rafters. "Daddy, if you're listening...we finally made it! This is for the both of us!" He smiles wide and stuffs the good luck charm back into his shirt, reaching for some talcum powder in the small bag attached to the side of his rodeo garb. He digs a thick handful out of the bag and raises his hand over his head. The crowd knows what's coming next...

Daryl smacks his hands together! White talcum powder bursts into the air exploding in front of him. The crowd roars even louder, stomping, clapping, and chanting. "Slap them bulls! Slap them bulls!" Daryl gets into his bullfighter stance; he gives two thumbs up to the two other bullfighters. "Let's do this!" shouting toward Blake and Bobby. The ABR rodeo announcer, aged mid-forties, tall with a nice brown mustache, stands above Christy and Cody in the announcer's booth over the arena floor. He's ready to get the ball rolling. This is the best bull riding event on the planet.

"Cowboys and cowgirls! Ladies and gentlemen!" he teases the crowd. "I hope you're ready for the best bull riders and bullfighters...innn theee wwooorrrlllddd!"

George Thorogood's crushing hit song *"Bad to The Bone"* starts playing over the loudspeakers:

"Bad to the bone, bad to the bone... Bbbbbaaaadd to the bone!"

The crowd is cheering and clapping, they are loving every moment. The rodeo announcer turns up the song higher, it blares over the loudspeakers. Daryl repositions himself in his stance again. The two other bullfighters get ready. Boom! The first bucking chute gate flies open! The action is fast and furious, one of the best bull riders in the world riding one of the toughest badass bulls in the world. The Latino bull rider, aged twenty-eight, small and wiry, is sticking like glue to his seat. The massive bull, almost the size of a small house, is bucking and twisting and turning sharp.

Daryl and the other bullfighters are immediately on the spot, dancing with the bull and keeping him contained to one area…four seconds…five seconds…six seconds…Daryl is flanking the big beast, keeping him in his sight. Blake and Bobby are circling around the monster…seven seconds…eight seconds…the buzzer wails loud.

A great ride! the Latino bull rider is tossed into the dirt. The bull angered, wanting to hit something, turns and spins, starting toward the Latino bull rider, who is just getting himself up from his fall. He tries to run toward the arena fence, stumbling and falls back into the thick dirt. Daryl dashes in between the wild bull and Latino bull rider, he gets the angry bull to follow him. He sidesteps left, then twists and turns, the big bull blinded by his rage. Blake now dashing in front, then Bobby rushing past him. The bull is confused and twisting all around. Spinning in circles.

Daryl leaps to the side, the bull swings around again. Daryl pivots and raises his white-covered hand, the crowd cheering. Daryl slaps the bull on his ass! Talcum powder burst! The crowd cheering and chanting crazy with bull fever. "Slap them bulls! Slap them bulls!"

Daryl high-fives Bobby, looking above the arena floor, he finds Christy and Cody standing in the wild throng of the crowd's bull fever. Christy throws Daryl a kiss. Cody has his fist raised chanting with the crowd "Slap them bulls! Slap them bulls!" Blake and Bobby lead the bull from the arena, jumping on the fence near the livestock exit gate, as the beast runs back into the bull pens behind the arena.

Daryl raises his fist and pumps it in the air. More cheers and shouts. He looks toward the second bucking chute. Rex is loading on the next bull. He sees Daryl and gives him a smug look. Tightening his hand around the bull cinch. Rex is here to win the World Championships.

The bull bursts from the gate! Rex riding like a pro on top, sticking and twisting with the large beast. Daryl positions around the bull, fighting the monster, trying to let Rex ride him. Blake and Bobby do their magic as well, dashing around and dancing with the ornery bull, who is throwing his head sideways and twisting around with a ton of fury. He's trying to hook Rex with his wide and jagged horns. Rex is sticking tight…four seconds…five seconds…six seconds… The bull is now jumping and twisting harder, you can see the strain on Rex's face. His eyebrows are crushed together, his breathing measured, every muscle in his upper body straining against the giant monster underneath him.

Christy and Cody are watching. Christy is confident that Daryl will keep her brother safe. Seven seconds… bull spins hard left…eight seconds…Rex is slipping, the arena buzzer wails loud. Rex clears the time, a great ride, the bull launches him about three feet into the air. Rex flies high, landing into the soft dirt on his feet, he drops and rolls away. Then immediately jumps up and starts for the arena fence.

The bull is right behind him, almost touching him. Daryl rushes to the side of the bull and touches him on the head, the monster of an animal turning toward Daryl.

Rex reaches the arena fence and jumps on the rails, climbing to the top and catching his breath. He's watching Daryl fight the big bull. Daryl dodges left, then cuts back right, the bull charges past. Daryl spins around and raises his white hand again. Slapping the bull on the ass! The crowd is going wild! Rex is watching Daryl. He's not as impressed as the crowd. He thinks it's all a joke and shakes his head in disgust. He drops over the other side of the arena fence into the contestant area, easily dropping on his two feet. Daryl and the other bullfighters get the big bull to follow them to the livestock exit gate.

The bull leaving the arena.

————

IT'S THE END OF A LONG NIGHT. DAY ONE OF THE WORLD Championships rodeo is over. The contestant staging area is full of reporters and bull riders, all doing post-show interviews. Blake and Bobby enter the area from the rodeo arena and walk among the bull riders in the staging area. They receive several warm thank you and nice job comments thrown their way from the contestants they helped keep safe. Most of the bull riders offer appreciative handshakes and firm slaps on the back for their fine work. The two bullfighters did a great job today and their work is very much appreciated. The rodeo camera crews are getting all the congratulations on live television.

Daryl follows Blake and Bobby about several feet back entering through the contestant's gate from the rodeo arena. His white powdered hands hang loose at his sides. His painted red, white, and blue face is getting attention. A pretty, young female reporter, early thirties, with dark red hair, steps in front of Daryl. Her camera team is already lighting Daryl up and rolling the scene. The lights are very bright and are blinding Daryl. He throws one of his talcum-powdered hands up to block the glare.

"Daryl, you were terrific tonight! The crowd loved you! How was the bullfighting out there?" the female reporter shoves her microphone into Daryl's face. He looks at the camera for a moment.

"It felt really good. Working with the best riders and the best bulls."

"The fans love you. 'Slap the Bulls!' is a giant hit. How did that all start?"

Daryl smiles then laughs. "Well, I got lucky with that one—"

Rex suddenly shoves his way in front of the camera. Pushes Daryl right in front of the live broadcast. "I almost lost my seat because of you, Weathers! Stay away from my bulls! Do you hear me!" He stands face-to-face with Daryl, who is staring back at Rex, he wants to hit him, but knows he can't do that right now, not here. "You don't belong in Las Vegas! You don't belong with my sister and her son! Only real cowboys and bull-fighters make the World Championships!" Rex is pushing against Daryl, who is clenching his fists. He wants to tell Rex he's wrong, that he's a dinosaur, a fungus that won't heal. The camera crew is all over them. The other bull riders and bullfighters are now watching the exchange.

Daryl stares at Rex. The cameras are watching him close, rolling live. Daryl grins and steps toward Rex and slaps him across the shoulders! White talcum powder spray fills the air behind Rex. "I love you too, Rex! You're one of the best bull riders in the entire sport! I'm a huge fan!" He smiles and pushes past the female reporter and her camera team with a giant grin sitting on his face.

There's a huge white powder handprint on Rex's back! Just like on the bulls' butts!

One of the camera crew picks up the white handprint and now flashes it across the big-screen over the arena floor. Everyone in the stadium can see the white mark left by Daryl on Rex. The remaining crowd are all looking up, now cheering and clapping loudly.

Daryl standing a short distance away is all smiles. He raises his white talcum powder hands and smacks them together. White powder mist explodes in the air. More cheers and shouts from the crowd. He sees Christy and Cody near the contestant area exit gate and starts walking toward them. Clearing his conscience of Rex, his old nemesis. He's happily married to a woman he loves and has a new son he adores.

Rex is trying to figure out what all the cheering and clapping is about. He looks up and sees the big-screen overhead. Several of the bull riders and Blake and Bobby are laughing out loud. Rex reaches behind his shirt and touches the white handprint. His face is turning red with embarrassment.

———

MID-MORNING AT THE SOUTH POINT HOTEL & CASINO. Daryl is sitting alone in a decorated outdoor café inside the large hotel at a table with a light blue tablecloth covering the top. The round table is set up with four seats. Daryl is waiting for Christy and Cody to meet him for breakfast. The café is open to the casino floor and there is a large crowd of rodeo fans, both cowboys and cowgirls, some with children, moving through the ground floor of the hotel. Daryl picks up a cup of coffee off the table and takes a long sip. It's a different world now from the whiskey he used to sip and drink.

He watches a cowboy about his age, and his son about Cody's age, playing together across the casino floor. The cowboy is trying to show his son how to build a rodeo loop and throw it through the air. They're keeping clear of the other guests in the hotel, the dad roping a small stone statue near one of the kiosks on the casino floor. Security hasn't noticed.

Christy and Cody appear moving through the crowd. Christy is holding Cody's hand to not lose him in the large mass of rodeo fans. Daryl now sees them and waves toward them, setting his coffee cup down. Daryl suddenly sees Tommy walking behind Christy and Cody and he's a bit surprised. Christy points toward Daryl at the table. Tommy now sees him there. They all start moving across the floor through the heavy crowd of hotel guests toward Daryl. Who stands before they arrive.

Christy comes up first with Cody in tow. "Before you get mad, it was my idea to invite your brother here to watch you fight the bulls."

Daryl faces Tommy and glares into his eyes. Tommy is accepting the challenge. The brothers haven't seen each other since the night Daryl ran into the ranch porch steps. There's a tense moment, neither sure what to say, then Tommy steps forward and grabs Daryl at the shoulders. Giving him a fast hug and slapping him across the back.

"Hey, dumbshit."

"Hey, jackass."

They say their old familiar greeting to each other. Daryl hugs Tommy tighter, slapping him across the back as well. Christy and Cody are smiling together, glad to see the brothers are accepting each other. The brother's unfavorable past is behind them. Tommy releases Daryl.

"So, ya went and got yerself married, huh? Didn't even invite your own brother?"

"We didn't invite anyone. I'm still surprised she said yes."

He leans over and kisses Christy whose smiling. Cody is laughing and shaking his head.

Tommy has some good news. "Rory moved his family onto the ranch. I gave him the spot near the pond."

"That was Daddy's favorite location." Daryl is looking at him.

"Yep, I know that." Tommy is smiling at him. He can't believe he's actually here talking with his little brother, now a professional bullfighter in the big leagues. His eyes set on Daryl a little closer. "I'm proud of you, brother. And I know Daddy would be too."

"Thanks, Tommy." Daryl grabs him in another tight hug, relieved that they are family again.

The man across the way finally gets his son to swing the lasso. The boy swings the rope over his head and releases, catching his dad. Cody sees it and laughs. Daryl cracks a smile.

He looks back at Tommy. "Think there might be room on the ranch for one more family when this thing is over? Just until the next season starts of course." He's laughing now.

Tommy is grinning wide. "I'm sure we can work something out." He watches Daryl. "Remember when we use to sleep in the barn as kids."

"That was fun." Daryl is grinning.

"Daddy would find us out there buried in the hay pile…"

"And pile more on top of us." Daryl laughs. They watch each other. "I miss him."

"Me too." Tommy is being sincere.

"I'm hungry, Momma." Cody is ready for breakfast.

"Ugh, I'm still raising a little monster."

"Here, everyone have a seat." Daryl pulls two chairs out for Christy and Cody. Tommy pulls his own chair out.

"Does he have to eat all the time?" Christy teases and rubs Cody's head as he drops in his chair.

"All the time." Daryl smiles, sitting across from them.

"I like eating." Cody watches the son across the casino floor rope his father again. "I wanna learn to rope like that. Will you teach me?" he asks Daryl.

"I can teach you." Tommy sits back and looks at Cody. "I'm better at using a rope than your new daddy. I work with a rope." He's grinning.

"Really?" Cody is excited.

"Yep. On the ranch." Tommy is still grinning; he looks over at Daryl.

Daryl grins back and high-fives Tommy.

"He's definitely a better roper than me."

Everyone is laughing now.

Cody knuckle-bumps Tommy. Who smiles back at him.

Daryl's new family is his family.

———

RODEO MUSIC PLAYS OVER DARYL FIGHTING MORE BULLS IN the T-Mobile Arena. The ABR World Championships of bull riding and bullfighting are pushing ahead day by day. Daryl saves several bull riders from some very nasty bulls. Daryl is slapping most of the bulls he's fighting on the ass with his trademark white talcum powder handprint. The rodeo crowds are cheering and clapping their excited approval. The shouts of support are rancorous and aggressive, almost as aggressive as the bullfighters themselves dodging and fighting the massive bulls in the rodeo arena.

"Slap them bulls! Slap them bulls!" The chanting continues throughout the championship series. The sports stations and reporters are eagerly covering every part of the action, their interviews with bull riders and the bullfighters are the best yet.

Christy and Cody watch each event from their seats below the rodeo announcer's booth. They are totally hooked on the world championship event. Christy can't believe that Daryl is so natural in the arena and completely at home each night for every go-round. Even at this level of bullfighting. Tommy is just as amazed. He decided not to fly back home to the ranch and stayed to watch the action. Rory and Sarah Jane are handling the ranch chores while he's in Las Vegas.

Daryl dodges a tough and mean-spirited Mexican bull, the smaller critter, turning sharp as a knife with double-sided blades, spinning back and forth. Daryl is just out of reach. He suddenly grabs the bull around the horns and lets the angry little fellow toss him up and over his back. Daryl expecting every movement, flips in the air and drops behind the bull, slapping him right on the ass! The rodeo crowd is completely enthralled and wild about their new bullfighter. He's leading the bullfighting World Championships scoring.

The next night and another bull with another white handprint. That's twelve for the World Championships series thus far. Daryl fights a rough bull that Rex has just rode and jumped off, after landing on his feet. The big beast starts to fight Daryl, then trots to the exit gate to the livestock pens. Daryl swaggers through the arena in the soft ankle-deep dirt. Rex walks past him toward the contestant exit gate, giving Daryl a look of disdain. Daryl ignores him, Rex isn't worth the attention, not in front of this crowd.

Blake and Bobby, and the two other backup bullfighters, Ryan and Jeramie, all converge in the arena together. Everyone is congratulating each other on another great night of work. The rodeo announcer, the same professional man in the announcer booth from the day one event, presents to the crowd with the bullfighter's scores as they are posted on the big-screen hanging above the stadium floor.

The three primary bullfighters, Daryl, Blake, and Bobby, pop up in sequence from #1 to #3 in the standings. Daryl has a commanding lead over the other two bullfighters. The crowd is cheering and clapping loudly, the other bullfighters are all high fiving him; they are all proud of him.

There's nothing here in the rodeo arena about personal egos or attitudes. It's about doing your best and keeping the bull riders and bullfighters safe. The champion bullfighter is a title that is earned, but at a great risk. Anyone of the bullfighters could be dangerously hurt and maimed in a matter of moments.

Christy watches Rex showing no respect for Daryl when he leaves the arena. She still feels that Daryl is doing a great job keeping her brother safe. She's greatly disappointed that Rex is holding such an ugly grudge toward Daryl and is a little angry at her brother. She watches Daryl high-five the other bullfighters as they prepare for the last bull ride of the night.

She looks over at Cody, who is shouting and yelling

his approval with the rest of the rodeo crowd. Christy's smile is genuine and real. She's proud of Daryl and his feelings for Cody.

Tommy, sitting next to them in their seats, is watching the entire action on the big arena floor. He looks at the bullfighter ratings on the big overhead screen. He still can't believe that his little brother is going to be a world champion! Bull rider to bullfighter!

He's still amazed.

18

SLAP THEM BULLS!

T-MOBILE ARENA—LAS VEGAS, NEVADA

FINAL NIGHT OF ACTION.

The last showdown in the rodeo arena between the dangerous bulls and the bull riders and bullfighters. There are thousands of occupied seats, the T-Mobile Arena stadium is filled to capacity and overflowing. Many of the spectators are standing, there's not enough seats for everyone. But the cowboys and cowgirls don't mind. They are here to watch the best of the best competing tonight and witness the American Bull Riders Association crowning of their world champion bull rider and bullfighter.

The vendors are even extra busy, with long lines forming all around the lower and middle stadium areas above the arena floor. A television sports commentator, aged in his early forties, with short, cropped hair and light beard, stands in the announcer's booth across the room from the primary rodeo announcer. Camera operator gets his focus aligned together and gives the television commentator a thumbs up, he's going live in three, two, one…

"Hello, rodeo fans! We're live again at the most dangerous show on earth! From Las Vegas, Nevada, it's the final night of the bull riding and bullfighting competition event of the year! The American Bull Riders and Bullfighters World Championships!"

The cameraman holds his aim on the commentator for another couple moments, then signals that they are off the air for the next sixty seconds, while the commentators back at the main television studio headquarters add their comments to the big event.

Down near the main arena, Christy and Cody approach Daryl, he's dressed in his bullfighting gear and wears the silver necklace and jeweled cross around his neck. His face is painted red, white, and blue again. Daryl's back is toward them, as they walk up to him. He turns; he's holding a new small black cowboy hat. He grins and pulls Cody's old beat-up cowboy hat off his head and sticks the new hat over Cody's ears, patting it down. "There ya go, Cowboy. Just what the doctor ordered."

"Where did you get this?" Cody pulls the hat off and checks it out, it's got a nice ribbon band around the rim. "This is way cool!" He plops the hat back on his head backward. Daryl laughs and resets it correctly the point of the brim forward.

"That's a great look, kiddo," Daryl teases him.

"Wow, a real cowboy hat." Christy is smiling.

"Is this really for me?" Cody is excited.

"Heck yes, you earned it." Daryl squeezes him on the shoulders.

"Thank you, Daryl!" Cody hugs him like he's his own father. Daryl squeezes him back, he surely feels Cody is his son now. He looks at Christy, who nods her thank you.

Rex is standing across the contestant's area watching them all together. Daryl sees him now. Rex looks like he hates Daryl. Christy sees Rex now as well. She's disappointed in his continued negative attitude and not happy about it. "Just ignore him, please."

"No problem." Daryl smiles at her. Tommy approaches with his two hands piled full of fresh hot dogs. He glances back up at the scoreboard overhead, Daryl still has a commanding lead in the bullfighting.

"I wish you'd hurry up and win this thing." He's grinning. Cody is already grabbing a hot dog with mustard.

"I bet these aren't as good as Mom's hot dogs."

Daryl and Christy laugh together.

"I'm working on it." Daryl slaps Tommy across the shoulder, answering his remark.

"One bull at a time, I get it." Tommy grins again and looks at Cody, who's already eating his hot dog. "I like your new hat, Cowboy."

"Daryl got it for me." Mouthful of hot dog stuffed down his throat.

"You're already spoiling him good, huh?" Tommy laughs. "We'll go get our seats if we can get through this heavy crowd." He grins and carries the hot dogs away, Cody follows him, still munching on his first hot dog.

Christy grabs Daryl and pulls him closer. "Come here, my bullfighter..." She kisses him and looks at him with genuine concern. "Please be safe out there. Okay?"

"Of course, I will." He kisses her back. Rex is watching them again from across the contestant's area, he shakes his head and turns away.

The rodeo announcer sticks his microphone up to his lips. " Alright cowboys and cowgirls!" He steps to the edge of the announcer's booth leaning out the open window and viewing down all around the over-filled stadium. "Tonight, we crown our world champion bull rider and bullfighter! Let's let them know how much we appreciate their efforts!" The crowd roars to life, clapping and cheering. Tommy and Cody have just reached their seats and plop down. Daryl sees them from where he is standing.

They're great seats, looking right over the action. He has a soft smile on his face and turns toward Christy. "There's a little stream on the ranch, with some big oak trees that would be a great place to build our home." He watches her. "Somewhere nice we could live a long time together and raise our family."

Christy stares back at him, her arms wrapped around his neck. "I'd like that."

"Maybe we could add a couple more kids...at least one more." Daryl is teasing her. He smiles wide, completely enamored with her. "I want to spend the rest of my life with you, Christy. You know that."

"Yes, I do." Christy is all smiles.

Daryl kisses her one more time, then knows it's time to get his head wrapped around the bull riding finals and start fighting bulls. Blake and Bobby are already in the rodeo arena, loosening up. The two backup bullfighters, Ryan and Jeramie, are also loosening up at the other end of the arena. Tonight, there are also two pickup men on horseback at the other end of the arena near the backup bullfighters for additional safety. They are the last line of defense if one of the three primary bullfighters, or the backup bullfighters, get injured and hurt.

Daryl looks at Christy. She gives him a wonderful smile and kisses him one more time, then steps away. The fans are cheering and shouting wildly, ready for the final bull riding event action to start. Daryl holds Christy's hand another moment, as she steps away, her soft fingers with the wedding ring slipping lovingly from his hand, as he lets her go.

"Wait for me. This will be over sooner than later. I'm excited about where this is going tonight." He nods at her, expecting the world championship, as she steps backward.

"Be safe out there." Christy smiles cheerfully and watches him one more moment, then turns away.

Daryl knows it's time to get into the rodeo arena. He moves toward the arena fence, slipping through the slats and jogging toward Blake and Bobby. The crowd erupts in louder cheers, shouting enthusiastically, "Slap them bulls! Slap them bulls!" Daryl joins the two other bull-fighters, grabbing a handful of white talcum powder from the bag at his waist and raises his hands high. Slapping them together in front of him, the talcum powder exploding in another flash of dust and vapor.

The crowd is roaring higher and louder. Daryl high-fives Blake and Bobby, more powder bursts, they all move to their fighting positions in front of the bucking chutes. Christy is watching from the stands as she moves toward her empty seat where Tommy and Cody are sitting.

The television sports commentator in the announcer's booth is back live on camera. He glances up at the big-screen above the arena floor. "Here's a quick look at our scoreboard leaders. Five-time American Bull Riders World Championship qualifier, Rex Winslow, is holding on to first place in the bull riding event. And first time ABR World Championship qualifier, Daryl Weathers, has a commanding lead in the bullfighter's event. Daryl used to ride bulls, what a change he's made!"

Daryl and the other bullfighters are standing ready in their fighting positions. The crowd is still aggressively shouting, "Slap them bulls! Slap them bulls!" Daryl can feel the importance of the moment and knows that he has made a major impact on the bullfighting sport. The rodeo announcer is on his feet again standing near the television sports commentator. "What a great night it's going to be!" The commentator nods his head toward him. He's back on standby for another sixty seconds. The rodeo announcer smiles and turns toward the open stadium, shouting out to the crowd in his microphone. "Leeett's get ready tooo riiide!"

Crowd is still chanting, "Slap them bulls! Slap them bulls!"

One of the cameras on the ground finds Rex. He's rubbing rosin on his bull-riding strap. He sees his face on the big-screen overhead; he's not at all excited. He sees Daryl standing in the center of the three bullfighters in the arena, waiting for the first bull of the night. He doesn't like Daryl but is realizing how much he actually likes his bullfighting skills. Though he won't let Daryl or Christy know that.

Daryl digs his cleats into the soft arena dirt. Something he's done now almost a hundred times before. He finds the hard surface under the loose dirt. The crowd noise is beginning to fade away, becoming a distant background in his mind. Daryl is focused now, his breathing shallows, he digs his hand back into the white talcum powder bag at his waist again, grabbing another handful and rubbing it onto both hands.

The bucking chute gate flies open!

Snot and fury is unleashed! A huge bull crashing forward, Bandy's Bad Boy, kicking and bucking. Trying to shake loose the young bull rider on his back, who is hanging on with all his might. This is his last chance of the year to win some of the prize money.

The bull is spinning left…non-stop like a cordless top on steroids…four seconds…five seconds…the bull rider is leaning hard right trying to counter the wild spinning. He's beginning to lose his seat…six seconds…the bull rider becomes unglued and is quickly thrown into the air. He comes crashing down hard onto the arena floor, Bandy's Bad Boy winning the matchup. Daryl charges forward, the two other bullfighters trying to help contain the massive beast, the bull is still spinning around. Then turns and charges straight for Daryl, who darts outside, the bull missing him, as Blake rushes past distracting the beast.

The bull is now following Blake, as Bobby dashes alongside the animal, confusing the bull, who turns and goes after Bobby then stops. Daryl speeds around the giant monster and leaps into the air, coming down on the other side and slapping the bull on the hind side! White talcum powder burst handprint! The crowd is screaming in pure delight and excitement. "Slap them bulls! Slap them bulls!"

Christy, Cody, and Tommy are all standing and screaming and shouting with the crowd. "Slap them bulls! Slap them bulls!" Cody is standing on his seat, looking over the taller man and his wife standing in the row in front of them. No one is sitting down, everyone in the stadium is standing and cheering, shouting loud and pumping their fists high in the air.

The two backup bullfighters, Ryan and Jeramie, move into the arena, getting Bandy's Bad Boy's attention, he chases them toward the livestock exit gate. A big white handprint planted right on his wide butt! The rodeo announcer is standing at the open window watching all the excitement. "Bandy's Bad Boy just made Chet Jackson's night a little lonelier!" He waits for the scoreboard big-screen above the arena floor to light up. A big zero. "Sorry, but no score! See ya next year, Chet!"

Chet, the young bull rider just thrown, is moving toward the contestant's gate, he's shaking his head, disappointed. Daryl walks toward him. "That was a good ride, no one could have rode him like that."

"Thanks, Daryl, I appreciate it." Chet shakes Daryl's hand. "And thanks for keeping him away from me."

"That's my job, what we do best." Daryl grins at him with his red, white, and blue painted face. He turns and trots over to the bucking chutes getting back in position again.

Blake and Bobby are in their places, scraping the soft dirt away, getting ready for another bull. The backup bullfighters, Ryan and Jeramie, are on the other side of the rodeo arena again.

The next bull rider, a short, thin Black rider, in his late twenties, stands on the bucking chute fence and cinches up his gloved hand with a leather covering. He waits for the bull in the chute to settle down, then climbs off the fence and onto the back of the large bull, wrapping the bull cinch around his gloved hand. The bull has two wide horns and throws his head a little. The chute crew tighten the rear cinch on the beast, it shuffles uneasy, the Black bull rider waits a moment, then nods to the gate man—

The gate swings open!

Another two thousand pounds of anger and aggression are unleashed! Bucking and spinning, jumping, kicking, trying to dislodge the Black bull rider on his back. Blake dashes at him first, the bull tries to gore him. Bobby runs up from the other side and grabs his tail, the crowd roaring their approval, classic rodeo bullfighting. Daryl slips between the bull and the chutes, dodging and dashing around the head of the horned beast.

The crowd is screaming with excitement...five seconds...six seconds...the Black bull rider is slipping, then regains his seat! Seven seconds...the bull is wild with anger, trying to get the rider off his back...eight seconds, the arena buzzer wails loudly, the crowd clapping, yelling and cheering. A solid ride.

The Black bull rider gracefully leaps off the monster and lands in the soft dirt. He starts running toward the arena fence, the bull turning to chase him. Daryl and the two other bullfighters are outplaying the large beast. Daryl spins out of the way and slaps the beast on the head! White powder handprint between his horns! Something new, the crowd loves it! The rodeo announcer leans out the open window in the announcer's booth and hits his full stride.

"Ladies and gentlemen, we got a tie score! Bulls one, Cowboys one..." He's smiling and cheering for the Black bull rider, the crowd is clapping their approval, it was a nice ride. Daryl and Bobby work the bull into the middle of the arena toward the back, the two backup bullfighters, Ryan and Jeramie, rush in to help get the bull to the livestock exit gate. Daryl and Bobby wait a moment, then turn away, as the two others get the large bull out through the gate.

The two bullfighters make their way back to the bucking chutes. Both standing in front with Blake. The rodeo announcer sees the score flash on the big-screen over the arena floor. Eighty-one points, a great ride. "Eighty-one points for Antonio Brown! We have a new go-round leader!"

Daryl and the two other bullfighters, Blake and

Bobby, high-five each other. They trot back to their starting positions, Daryl standing in the middle. The crowd is clapping and cheering their approval with genuine appreciation. Christy, Cody, and Tommy are still standing at their seats, Cody is still jumping up and down on his seat. Daryl looks up at them and Christy waves to him. She throws him a kiss.

Daryl 'catches' his wife's kiss and lovingly pats it on his painted cheek. Christy has a big smile. Cody and the audience are watching the replay overhead on the big-screen. Daryl spinning around and slapping the last bull on his head with a big white handprint. The crowd cheers and shouts some more.

Daryl looks back up into the seats and throws a kiss back to Christy, she grabs it in her hand and holds it. Then putting it close to her heart. Daryl loves it all, he's feeling good tonight. There's about ten more bull riders and the World Championships are done for the year. He sees the bullfighting update on the scoreboard overhead. He still has a nice, large lead. There's a feeling of final accomplishment. The World Championship is within his grasp. Blake and Bobby are settled into their starting positions, they both give Daryl a thumbs up. He glances toward the bucking chutes.

Rex is standing over one of the chutes pulling his riding glove over his fingers and getting ready to load up on his bull. He looks across the arena at Daryl. He sees Christy looking at him from the stadium seats. She's got her hands clasped together hoping for the best for her brother. Rex knows she has always supported him. It's his sister. He looks back at Daryl, then unexpectedly gives Daryl a thumbs up.

Christy and Daryl, both see it. Christy opens up with a warm smile. Daryl sees her expression, he knows she loves her brother and has always respected him. Daryl isn't sure the thumbs up was for him or Rex himself. He looks at Rex one more time, Rex nods his head and smiles. Daryl knows it was for him. He digs his cleats deeper into the soft dirt.

Rex steps off the bucking chute gate and loads on top of the massive white bull standing underneath him in the bucking chute. It's a monster of a beast, bigger than all of the other bulls in the World Championships rodeo. An albino freak of nature, with one broken horn, his left horn, shaped like an eight-inch meat cleaver, sharp and dangerous around the edges. The animal has a big black spot on its forehead.

Daryl now sees the broken left horn. Visions of his father's career ending wreck many years ago are coming back to his mind. He takes a shallow breath and ignores it.

19

FINAL SHOWDOWN

DARYL CLEARS HIS MEMORY. THE VISION OF HIS FATHER'S bad wreck is in the past. This is today, right now, at this moment in time. The past doesn't matter right now.

Rex sits on top of the albino freak of nature, the monster under him is not happy, it paws and digs at the dirt. The chute crew cinches down the rear bull strap, the big beast snorts louder and paws harder, moving its broken horn around in the front of the chute. Then it bashes the broken horn against the chute gate. The rodeo announcer standing overhead is watching the entire setup below him.

"Up next, our scoreboard leader in the bull riding competition, Rex Winslow…" The crowd offers loud cheering and clapping. The announcer is watching the large white bull in the bucking chute stomp and snort, unsettled and agitated. "Our points leader is riding one of the toughest bulls on the rodeo circuit, Final Justice. An aptly given name." The rodeo announcer knows the bull has never been ridden before in any ABR competition. He starts to announce that fact to the crowd, then decides not to mention it.

The dark black mark on the bull's albino face stands out in the bucking chute. Rex is having a tough time getting the beast to settle down, it doesn't want to calm. It suddenly tries to climb out of the chute box, its front legs reaching over the chute gate, the chute crew reacting quickly and getting the bull back down into the box. Rex is sitting tight on its back, hanging on, trying not to fall under the bull into the bucking chute. He knows if he rides this monster, he will win the World Championships. It's one of the toughest rides he has sat on for a long while.

The agitated bull settles just enough for Rex to finally get a good seat on the albino's back. Daryl is watching the entire action inside the bucking chute from his bull-fighter position on the floor of the rodeo arena. He knows this is going to be a tough bull to fight. Rex is one of the best bull riders. But it's going to be a strong match up.

Rex tightens his hand one more time in the bull rope over the bull's back. Clenching it tighter than normal. He waits for a couple of beats and then tugs his hat down lower over his head. He exhales a deep breath, catching his wind, relaxing for the championship ride. He waits for another moment.

Then nods at the gate man.

The chute gate flies open!.

The massive white bull leaps from the open chute with Rex clutching hard to his back. He's expending every ounce of strength to stay on top. The white beast is jumping and snorting, tearing and ripping through time and space, violent and angry, kicking his rear hooves higher than the other bulls.

Daryl rushes forward to try and get the bull's attention. The giant animal is throwing arena dirt, snorting loud, thrashing its head sideways. Daryl is trying to stay away from the sharp broken horn, a large dagger looking to maim someone. Blake runs in toward the bull from the outside. The beast instinctively lowers its giant head and smashes Blake sideways, his head snapping back, throwing Blake against the arena fence! Blake lies there unconsciously.

Bobby comes in at the bull from the other side. Daryl is dodging the horns in the front, the bull automatically turns on Bobby, who tries to sidestep away, catching him from behind and tossing him fifteen feet into the air across the arena floor. Bobby hits the soft dirt and lies there a moment, stunned and trying to regain his senses. He rises to his knees…

The two backup bullfighters, Ryan and Jeramie, rush into the arena to help Daryl fight the bull. Rex is sitting on top, is trying to control the monster…four seconds… Daryl dashes around the white albino again, its head lowered, the dark black mark glaring at Daryl, the bull starts chasing him, spinning and turning faster than Daryl can run…five seconds…the large stadium crowd is screaming with support, stunned, now realizing this beast may be unstoppable…

Rex is coming unglued on top of the giant white bull, he's losing his seat, there's no way to hang onto this massive monster of destruction…Christy, Cody, and Tommy are watching from their stadium seats, also realizing that this is going to be a terrible ride for Rex. Christy grabs Cody and pulls him closer to her side. Cody's eyes are wide open.

The white bull is clearly in charge here. Blake still isn't moving on the arena floor near the fence, and

Bobby can't stand. He fractured his lower femur when he hit the dirt floor. He's trying to crawl away from the fight toward the arena fence opposite where Blake is lying unconscious. Several bull riders are reaching through the fence, trying to pull Blake out of the arena through the open slats.

Six seconds...the bull is chasing Daryl who is dodging and spinning. He's barely able to avoid the wide hooked right horn and the broken sharp left horn. He turns toward the arena fence, Ryan and Jeramie arrive on the scene and try to get the bull's attention. The bull turns toward Bobby crawling toward the arena fence. Daryl dashes back between them, trying to distract the crazy monster.

Rex can't hang on much longer, he now realizes his hand is stuck in the bull cinch. Ryan and Jeramie rush toward the white albino, the beast spins like a dime and smashes Ryan in the ribs, there's a loud cracking sound, his sternum breaking. The beast slams Ryan sideways again, throwing him against Jeramie, they hit their heads hard together hard, knocking them both almost senseless. Both fall into the dirt.

Seven seconds...Daryl is the only bullfighter standing on his feet. Rex has lost his seat, he slips off the side of the beast of fury, his hand is stuck in the bull rope, the white monster jumps and kicks. There's a noisy pop and crack, Rex screams in pain, his shoulder dislocated. The white bull starts smashing Rex with his massive head, beating Rex unconscious, hitting him with the hooked horn, but thank goodness missing him with the broken sharp horn.

Christy is terrified now; she's got her hands over her mouth. She's crying loudly, holding Cody close to her side, squeezing him too tight. Tommy is watching the deadly wreck, visions of his father's bad accident also in his mind. He sees Daryl alone in the arena...

Eight seconds...the arena buzzer wails away. The massive white albino bull is not done. He turns toward Daryl. Rex is hanging off the beast's side, completely knocked out. The two pickup men on horseback come charging into the arena with their lariats raised over their heads. Daryl charges straight for the white beast, he dodges his head and horns, grabbing the bull riding rope around its massive chest, trying to unhook the strap to free Rex, the rope is stuck tight. The white bull is trying to get to Daryl, who keeps dodging and spinning away. Rex is still unconscious on the other side, bleeding, bouncing, being jerked around, his shoulder out of the socket.

Tommy stands and leaves his seat. Working through the crowd standing in shock in the same row. He's moving toward the arena floor. Christy watches him leaving, she's looking at Daryl in the arena. Her brother hanging helplessly on the other side of the massive white bull.

Daryl finally gets the bull rope free. The white bull flings Rex's limp body across the arena. He lands in the soft dirt about fifteen feet away. The bull turns toward Daryl. Rodeo personnel are now in the arena pulling Bobby off the floor to safety. The bull riders have pulled the unconscious Blake through the arena fence slats and out of harm's way.

The two pickup men finally arrive at the bull and throw their lariats around his massive head and neck. They rope the huge albino bull trying to pull him out of the arena. The bull pulls back jerking them both almost out of their saddles. Then the monster turns and charges the closest horseman and gores his horse!

The giant beast lifts the terrified horse and rider into the air, tossing them both against the other horse and rider. Knocking both horses and both pickup men to the ground! The bull charges and runs over the two pickup men trying to get out from under their saddles cinched tight to their horses. The bull's hooves and head knocking both men out of their senses. They lay there unmoving!

Daryl stands alone. He's out of options. The massive bull, the size of a small truck, wants to crush him. The white bull squares off with him. Man versus beast.

Rex, conscious now, still dazed and confused, lifts himself from the dirt arena floor. He grabs his damaged arm, the pain is intense, he's starting to realize what happened. He is unaware of the danger still in the arena. The white bull sees Rex. Now his new target. The bull lowers his head and paws at the ground, turning toward Rex. The crowd is yelling at the arena crew to do something to help Rex and Daryl. The albino beast is clawing and scraping the ground, throwing dirt everywhere, getting ready to charge and smash right into Rex.

Daryl is still standing in the arena. He can run to the arena fence and escape the beast. Flee to safety, saving himself and live another day. Leaving Rex standing in the dirt on his own. He loves his wife and his new son. He wants to be with them forever.

Christy stares at Daryl. He looks up and sees her standing with Cody clutched tight to her side near their seats. Christy doesn't want her brother hurt but doesn't want Daryl hurt either. She loves her new husband very much. Tommy reaches the arena fence in the contestant area. He shouts from behind the fence at Daryl. "Get out of there! You can't win this fight!"

Daryl has but a moment to think. To save himself and

come back to his new wife and son. To abandon his life-long nemesis Rex for certain death. It's not Daryl's fault that Rex couldn't ride the albino monster. He didn't get on the bull, Rex did. Daryl stares at the white bull, his black mark on his forehead and his broken horn. The massive beast is clawing and snorting louder, tearing the ground up, nostrils flaring. It lowers its massive head again with the dark black mark and charges toward Rex!

Daryl doesn't wait. He starts running toward the bull. Realizing that he can't live with the guilt of Rex's death, if he is killed in front of his sister, Daryl's beautiful wife. Whom Daryl loves more than anything on earth. He won't be able to forgive himself. Not now, not ever. Just like his father's guilt about his own mother. Daryl sticks his hand in the white talcum powder bag hanging at his side. He runs in between the white bull and Rex, and leaps high into the air, coming down and slapping the white bull on the black spot on its forehead!

Loud smack! Talcum powder burst! White powder sprays everywhere in the arena air. The crowd is stunned and amazed, they never expected that. They're screaming and cheering, clapping and stomping, begging Daryl to get out of the arena. The white bull stops and spins around.

The fresh white handprint looks huge on his forehead!

The massive beast bellows loudly. Its angry roar filling the entire arena and stadium, bouncing off the rafters and ceiling. The full-house crowd is watching in terror and fear. The big beast drops its head again and aims at Daryl. It charges right for him. Faster than a racehorse, sprinting right at Daryl, who dodges and spins. The most amazing bullfighting ever witnessed!

Daryl is twisting and turning away, dashing around

the monster, trying to get him to move toward the live-stock exit gate. They run past the downed horses and incapacitated pickup men. They run past the two backup bullfighters. Jaime is dragging Ryan across the arena toward the fence. Ryan is seriously injured and only partially conscious. Jaime is also hurt, his nose is broken and bleeding. He can barely pull his friend out of the arena.

Daryl suddenly spins and gets behind the white bull. He raises his talcum-powdered hand high above his head, the crowd sees it coming. He yells and shouts and slaps the bull right on the ass! He's never slapped a bull twice! The stadium crowd is screaming and yelling at the top of their lungs. "Slap them bulls! Slap them bulls!" Daryl is fighting this beast like he owns him now. A true champion of the sport.

The giant bull is starting to get tired; he slows a half step. Daryl turns and dodges, the beast chases him toward the exit gate. Daryl is working him out of the arena. He's doing an amazing job fighting the white monster alone. He sprints and spins, dodging the animal one more time. Suddenly, Daryl's foot slips out from under him! His football cleat hitting the hard surface below the dirt. Daryl drops to the arena floor on one knee. The white albino lowers his head and gores Daryl with the broken horn!

Gouging him in the middle of the abdomen. Daryl's face registers shock and pain. The hit was deep and into his stomach. He's trying not to scream, to hold himself together in front of the world and get up and get this crazy animal out of the arena. The white monster lifts Daryl over his head and hurls him across the dirt. Then charges and headbutts him with the white handprint, sending Daryl rolling end over end across the arena floor. The animal charges again and smashes Daryl mercilessly against the fence, then finally stops. He snorts loudly and bellows, spraying Daryl with slime and spit. The white beast stands over Daryl. The slime dripping from his mouth.

Daryl, barely conscious, isn't moving. Rex is still standing in the arena about thirty feet away, frozen in his own tracks. He wants to charge the bull. He starts running toward him, holding his dislocated shoulder and arm. "Get outta here! Get outta here!" The white bull bellows again. Its bloody broken horn raised toward the crowd. They watch in complete silence. The beast turns and rushes toward Rex; it comes within two feet of hitting him hard, then runs right past him and out of the livestock gate, exiting the arena.

The arena floor is a strewn mess of destruction and chaos. Daryl is gored and mauled, bleeding heavy. Blake and Bobby hurt, the backup bullfighters, Jamie and Ryan, hurt, the two pickup men and their horses lying injured on the ground. Emergency technicians and rodeo personnel are running into the arena to help.

Rex standing in the dirt, realizes it's finally over. He starts limping toward Daryl, his damaged arm hanging at his side. He's shouting for help. "Get the medics over here! Hurry!" He drops over Daryl who lies there with his eyes open, he's barely breathing, his heartbeat is slowed. There's blood pooling in the thick dirt underneath him. "Hang in there, Daryl. They're coming to help."

Tommy comes into the arena and runs to Daryl. "You won, brother! You whipped that bull's ass!" Daryl can barely hear him talking. He's drifting away into a place of darkness and near death. The crowd is still quiet. Waiting and watching. Christy and Cody are making their way to the arena floor. Christy is crying. Cody is crying. They are in total shock. Emergency techs and bull riders come into the arena, helping the backup bull-fighters, the pickup men and their horses.

Two emergency personnel come to Daryl, getting between Rex and Tommy. They encourage Daryl to stay tough and don't give up because we can fix you, as they quickly assess his injuries and try to stop the bleeding from the deadly bull's broken horn that punctured his abdomen.

Daryl can feel his life leaving him behind. The arena floor underneath him begins to roll away. The heavy arena dirt moving past him, untethered, unrestricted.

Daryl sees a flashback.

His father, a younger Cal, standing over Daryl as a small boy, about age eight, sitting on a steer in the bucking chutes at the Texas ranch. The last rays of sunlight surrounding the father and son...the chute gate opens, and Daryl and the steer are released. The little bull running and bucking into the glowing rays of sunlight...Cal is smiling and shouting encouragement. "You got this, Daryl! You are going to be a champion one day!" Daryl is hanging on but then is thrown off. Cal is laughing and helping him to his feet, hugging him tight. "I love you, son! You're a natural!"

Daryl stares at the stadium roof way up high above the arena floor. The emergency technicians are still getting him prepared to take him to the hospital. A metal stretcher with rollers is standing at the contestant's exit gate across the heavy dirt. Rex and Tommy are watching Daryl closer now, they see him losing consciousness, they're praying, and hoping he's going to recover.

Daryl sees Cal standing above him. His father is close to him, gesturing, smiling, nodding his approval. "Great job, son. You're a world champion. Time to go now."

Daryl's face lightens into a slight smile. He hears his own words.

"We did it, Daddy..."

Emergency techs and Tommy are lifting Daryl off the ground onto a stretcher, carrying him toward the gurney with rollers at the exit gate. The medical personnel are still trying to stop the bleeding in his stomach, it's bad, the gash deep and violent. Christy is pushing her way through the chaos on the arena floor holding Cody's hand tight, she comes up to the group standing next to Daryl. She's still crying and sobbing. Trying to maintain control. Cody is still stunned and quiet, tears wet in his eyes. He looks at Daryl, he can't believe this happened to his new daddy. He loves Daryl.

Christy leans closer over Daryl; she's walking with the others. "I'm here, Daryl." She takes his hand, the white talcum powder spread across his palm and fingers. She presses his white hand against her cheek. Mixing the white powder with her tears of despair and fear. Daryl can barely hear or see her next to him. Yet he knows it's his beautiful wife, Christy, standing there, holding his hand. He tilts his head toward her, his face curls slightly at the edges into a soft smile. The best he can offer. His breathing is shallow now, almost nonexistent. His heart is barely beating. He squeezes Christy's hand back, then gasps and exhales. He becomes still. Christy is crying harder now.

The emergency techs reach the metal gurney with the stretcher. Tommy and the medics lifting Daryl on top, they strap him down. Rex steps toward Christy, he holds his sister with his good arm. "He's a good man, Christy. I should have told you that before."

Christy turns and cries against his chest. The emergency techs softly pull her away and move Rex toward the exit gate. He needs to get to the hospital as well.

Cody hugs his mother, watching Daryl being rolled away toward one of the ambulances. "Is he going to live, Mommy?" Christy turns to him and hugs him tighter. Her eyes are filled with tears, her happiness taken away. Tommy comes over to them both and offers comfort. He holds them like family, which they are now. The three of them turn and walk together toward the ambulances, following the emergency crew.

Shock and disbelief.

20

BIRTHDAY PARTY

BEAUTIFUL SUMMER AFTERNOON. SUNSHINE AND CLEAR blue skies with wisps of soft clouds rolling around the edges of the pastures and the rolling hills of the Weather's ranch. Cattle are grazing near the family cemetery with its nice green grass growing under the beautiful oak trees. We see three headstones standing side by side now. First is Calvin Weathers, second is Audrey Weathers, and a third headstone that we can't see the name engraved on the white slab of granite.

Now singing is heard around the outdoor back patio porch of the ranch house. There are several voices of all ages, adults and children alike. "Happy birthday to you! Happy birthday to you..."

Smoke billows over the back porch from the open cover of a large propane gas barbecue grill fired up and cooking hot dogs and hamburgers. There's a birthday cake on the patio table with white frosting and red and blue icing squeezed on the edges circling several rose-colored flowers embedded on top of the cake.

Nine rainbow-colored candles are lit up on the

birthday cake ready to be blown out. There are several wrapped gifts sitting around the cake on the patio table. Country music plays low in the background from an outdoor speaker.

Christy stands with Cody in front of the birthday cake. He wears the newer black cowboy hat that Daryl gave him. Christy is seven months pregnant. Her belly is showing the expectation of the new arrival soon. Happy Birthday, Cody is written across the birthday cake.

Tommy, Rex, Rory, Sarah Jane, and their two daughters, Ashley and Miranda, are all standing around the patio table with Cody and Christy. Everyone finishes the birthday song, *"Happy birthday to you...Cody!"*

Cody leans forward and with a big gasp of breath, blows out the birthday candles. Cheers and clapping from everyone. "Make a wish! Make a wish!" Ashley and Miranda jump up and down, excitedly shouting. There's more laughter and clapping.

Cody looks at the birthday cake. "I wish that my new baby sister is going to be beautiful like my mom!" He smiles at Christy and hugs her belly. Christy is smiling and softly laughing. She rubs Cody's shoulders and swats his cowboy hat down over his eyes. Cody pulls it back up, the two sisters, Ashley and Miranda, come over next to him, both eager to get a piece of birthday cake.

Cody grabs one of the gifts on the patio table. He starts to pull off the wrapping paper. Christy pushes a small box about the size of a cell phone, right in front of him. "Hang on...open this one first. It's from Daryl." She looks at Rex and Tommy, both shaking their heads with approval.

Christy glances toward the back glass sliding doors of the rear of the house, she looks down and touches her belly. "Your sister just kicked again." She looks at Cody, who grins and touches her firm belly; he feels another kick.

"She's going to be a cowgirl."

Christy laughs and covers her mouth. "Probably, so."

Cody looks at the small box with a quizzical look. Rex and Tommy already know what the gift is. Cody pulls the light wrapping paper off the gift. It's not a cell phone. It's a felt-covered jewelry case. Cody looks at Christy a little confused. "What is this?" He lifts the lid and opens the small jewelry box.

Inside there's a gold and silver inlaid rodeo belt buckle. American Bull Riders Association is engraved across the top of the buckle, with Daryl Weathers—World Champion Bullfighter engraved across the face and bottom of the belt buckle.

"This is really awesome!" Cody is surprised and all smiles. He touches the gorgeous buckle, his fingers tracing Daryl's name.

"He knew you would like this." Christy is smiling lovingly at Cody.

"That buckle's bigger than you are, Cowboy!" Rex high-fives his nephew.

"You're gonna need to add about fifty pounds to wear it!" Rory teases him.

"Just what we need, another bullfighter in the family." Tommy grabs him in a tight hug around the shoulders. The young girls are giggling and laughing. They grab a couple of birthday gifts and stack them in front of Cody.

"Where is Daddy, anyway?" Cody looks up from staring at the belt buckle.

As now, Daryl walks out the back glass sliding door!

"Hey, who wants ice cream with their cake?!"

"Me! Me! Me!" Ashley and Miranda have their hands raised high.

"Me, too!" Cody looks at the belt buckle one more time and sets it down.

"You already opened it? The belt buckle?" Daryl plops the bucket of ice cream down on the table and starts scooping big spoonfuls onto the plastic plates where the slices of cake will be laid.

"It was my idea." Christy kisses Daryl. She starts cutting the cake. "He was anxious to start opening his gifts." Daryl laughs. Rex grabs the ice cream bucket from Daryl.

"I like ice cream, too." They look at each other and laugh together. Rex picks up a spoon and starts digging into the dessert.

Christy touches her belly again. "Our baby is really excited today." She puts Daryl's hand on her belly. He feels the baby kicking.

"Miranda was like that. Always kicking, letting me know she was there." Sarah Jane touches her daughter Miranda on the shoulder, the young girl waiting for her cake and ice cream. She smiles and steps next to Christy. Daryl is putting the freshly cut slices of birthday cake on the plastic plates next to the scoops of ice cream. Rory is turning the hot dogs and hamburgers on the open barbecue grill.

Daryl puts his arm around Christy, holding the spatula he just served the cake with close to her face. "Want a taste of this delicious birthday cake?"

She laughs and grabs his hand, licking the spatula. Daryl kisses her and holds it for a moment, tasting the cake icing. "I love you." Christy is all smiles.

"I love you, too." She kisses him back, tenderly, happy he survived the terrible wreck in the arena. "Oh, I forgot to tell you. Mr. Flores called this morning. He wants you back in the arena next year."

"Do you really want me to fight bulls again?" Daryl holds her and looks at her closer.

"Not really," she teases him. "But you did kick that big white bull's ass and <u>you are</u> the World Champion." She's smiling wider. "You may have to defend your title."

"And my integrity…" Daryl kisses her again. They laugh together. "Maybe I'll fight some more bulls after our daughter is born." He squeezes her tighter, touching her belly again.

Cody tears the wrapping off more birthday gifts. Sarah Jane has handed the birthday cake and ice cream to the girls, who giggle and squeal with delight eating their treats and watching Cody open his gifts.

Garth Brooks's cowboy song, "Rodeo" starts playing on the outdoor speaker. Rex turns it up, knuckle-bumping Daryl, still digging into the ice cream bucket. Tommy sets the hot dogs and hamburgers on the table on a big open platter. Cody sets his cake and ice cream down and grabs the mustard and a hot dog. Spraying and covering his lunch. Everyone is laughing and feeling great.

"His eyes are cold and restless, his wounds have almost healed…and she'd give half of Texas, just to change the way he feels…"

The girls and Cody are munching on hot dogs and birthday cake. Rory and Sarah Jane kiss and hold each other. Rex and Tommy are both singing along to Garth Brooks's song like they know it by heart:

"She knows his loves in Tulsa, and she knows he's gonna go… Well it ain't no other woman's flesh and blood, it's that damned old rodeo…"

Daryl stares at everyone and his mind is fighting the bulls in the arena, running, turning, spinning, slapping the big beasts on their wide rear ends with big white talcum powder handprints. The crowd's going wild and shouting their approval.

"Well, it's bulls and blood, its dust and mud, it's the roar of the Sunday crowd... It's the white in his knuckles, the gold in his buckle, he'll win the next go 'round..."

Cody and the girls are dancing and jumping around, Tommy and Rex are dancing with them. Daryl is holding Christy's hand and stepping cowboy style together around the outdoor patio.

Rory and Sarah Jane are doing the same thing, standing close together, dancing, laughing and loving. Rex is still singing and eating his ice cream out of the bucket...

"It's boots and chaps, it's cowboy hats, it's spurs and latigo... It's the ropes and the reins, and the joy and the pain... and they call it rodeeooo..... ..."

Music and lyrics playing on the patio.

Daryl kisses Christy and holds it. Looking right into her eyes.

Now together forever...

A LOOK AT:
THE HARD RIDE

He survived the war, but the real fight was waiting in the West.

In the chaos of a lawless frontier, James Butler "Wild Bill" Hickok walks a deadly line between hero and outlaw. Scarred by years of brutal conflict and the weight of too many graves, he returns to the plains seeking peace only to find more bloodshed.

When Hickok meets Agnes Lake, a fiercely independent equestrian performer with a tragic past, their connection runs deep. But love offers no protection in towns like Hays City and Deadwood, where outlaws, rival factions, and hired guns rule the streets. As a newly minted sheriff, Hickok becomes both symbol and target.

As rival gunslingers close in and old enemies resurface, Hickok must navigate shifting alliances, violent confrontations, and a town teetering on the edge of chaos. Each decision brings him closer to the justice he swore to uphold—or the grave he's been outrunning for years.

With justice fading and vengeance rising, Hickok must confront the truth: redemption carries a price—and not everyone rides away clean.

AVAILABLE NOW

ABOUT THE AUTHOR

Award-winning producer, director, and screenwriter, Thadd Turner has directed, produced, and written over a dozen feature films. He won the 2010 Western Heritage Wrangler Award for the History Channel's series "Cowboys and Outlaws", he won the 2007 Western Heritage Wrangler Award for the film "Truce" and won the 2006 Western Writers of America Spur Award for his original screenplay "Miracle at Sage Creek" that he produced, starring David Carradine, Wes Studi, Michael Parks, Buck Taylor, and Irene Bedard. He directed country music star Clay Walker's "Jesse James" music video. Thadd has ten feature film screenplays in active development that he has written, including Buttermilk Sky, East of Yuma, Diamond Rose, Heaven is Home, Cross Country Cowboy, Texas Hold 'Em, Palominas, Gold Run, Johnny Kidd, and Wiggle Room. Thadd is a member of the Writers Guild of America, Screen Actors Guild, and Western Writers of America.

www.talmarcfilms.com/shop